The vines followed the contours of the rolling stretched way up into the distance. The track came to a T-junction with a signpost; it pointed in one direction to Montaud, which was two kilometres away, and in the other to Arbon, eight kilometres distant.

They stopped for a moment and put their cases down.

'The parting of the ways,' said Vivien, trying to make light of an important moment for both of them.

Emily gave Vivien a hug and looked up at her. Vivien saw that Emily was trembling.

'Be careful, now,' said Vivien.

'And you.'

'No drunken orgies, mind!'

A shadow of a smile crossed Emily's face.

'And you'd better powder down those cheeks before you get there,' added Vivien. 'Aren't you meant to have had TB?'

'See you tomorrow, as planned.'

'Yes, if I'm not completely crippled. Eight bloody kilometres!' exclaimed Vivien.

The two women hugged each other again, picked up their cases and set off in opposite directions.

Also in Arrow
WISH ME LUCK

WISH ME LUCK II

by Frances Heasman

ARROW BOOKS

Arrow Books Limited
62–65 Chandos Place, London WC2N 4NW

An imprint of Century Hutchinson Ltd

London Melbourne Sydney Auckland
Johannesburg and agencies throughout the world

First published 1989

Set in Times
by JH Graphics Ltd, Reading

Made and printed in Great Britain
by Anchor Press Limited
Tiptree, Essex

ISBN 0 09 965040 1

WISH ME LUCK II

CHAPTER 1

Marie looked around at the small crowd of townspeople. It must have been like this in the days of the guillotine, she thought. One of Marie's neighbours Annette – a stout woman in her forties – nodded pleasantly to her.

'Ready!' said the officer in charge.

Marie could feel the sweat on her face, smell her own fear and the fear of others. It was one of those airless summer days in south-west France, when you long for the weather to break.

The three British agents did not glance at each other as they stood with their backs against the high brick wall. They wore the clothes of French railway workers; but their disguise had failed them, and now the goods-yard in which they had worked was to be their place of execution. Two of them were barely in their twenties, although the other was older, stockier and more rugged: forty, perhaps, or more. Not that it matters, thought Marie; there is no escape for any of them.

'Aim!' As the soldiers stepped back and raised their rifles the three agents continued to stare straight ahead. Marie wiped her nose to hide the fact that her eyes were filling with tears.

'Fire!' ordered the German officer.

The three Englishmen fell to the ground. The officer

walked over to the motionless bodies and kicked each of them hard; then, satisfied that all were dead, he issued an order to his men. Marie expected that the bodies would be displayed to the villagers as an example: probably hung from the footbridge which crossed the railway line. That was the usual practice.

She hoped that no one had noticed her tears. To the end, the three men had shown no sign of recognizing anyone in the crowd, which was as it should be. Marie nodded briefly to Annette, did her best to smile and walked quickly back through the cobbled side-streets to her father's hardware shop. As she pushed the door open she was thankful to see the shop was empty of customers. She slammed the door behind her and the bell jangled.

'Coming!' an elderly male voice croaked from the back room.

Leon Ferrier was a tough, wiry old man in a wheelchair, embittered by many things but mostly by his disability. As he propelled himself through to the shop he looked at his daughter, already knowing the worst.

'They've shot them,' Marie told him.

'Bastards!' said the old man. 'A wonder they didn't round up half the town as well.'

'Two of them weren't much older than Luc.'

'I said they were taking too many risks.' Leon shrugged. 'Crazy English!'

'It's for us they were taking the risks, Papa,' Marie pointed out. 'We must get word to Louis.'

'Luc can go.'

Marie walked across the shop, which once had been full of every kind of utensil but now was a sorry sight. Four years of war had taken its toll on the stock of merchandise.

'Luc!' Marie called up the stairs.

*

'All three of them?' said Faith Ashley.

Nodding, Cad drew on his cigarette and stared out of his office window overlooking Baker Street and nodded. Then he tossed the message to Faith, who read it intently.

Each time she received news of an agent's death over in France, she thought she would be better able to bear it. Each time proved her wrong.

'Three of our best men too,' said Cad, angrily stubbing out his half-smoked cigarette. 'Christ!'

'How were they caught?' asked Faith.

'No one knows,' answered Cad helplessly. 'Bad security, I suppose . . . some bloody Gaullist talking too much!'

'The families will have to be told,' she sighed.

Cad nodded, and looked her straight in the eye.

'See to it, would you?' he said.

'Three?' asked Liz.

'I'm afraid so,' said Faith, opening the appropriate drawer of her filing cabinet and riffling through her agents' personal files.

'Once upon a time, one of them could have been me,' mused Liz.

'It could,' Faith agreed. 'Don't tell me you're missing active service.'

'No,' said Liz doubtfully.

Faith knew what Liz was going through. Many of the married women agents had difficulty in accommodating themselves to normal life once they had returned from France.

'Everything okay?' Faith asked, meaning between Liz and her husband Laurence.

'Oh, everything's settling down,' smiled Liz, 'as much as it can do in wartime, I mean.'

Faith placed the manilla folders on the table and sat opposite her.

'I'm afraid I shall have to leave it to you, Liz. I'm seeing recruits all day.'

'There had to be a first time,' said Liz nervously.

'There are only two next-of-kin to contact,' Faith informed her in a businesslike manner. 'Bob Mattingly didn't want his mother told; she's very ill.'

Liz knew what that meant. The letters home which Bob had written before leaving for France would continue to be delivered.

'Donald Cooper's parents live in Scotland – you'll have to telephone them.'

Liz grimaced. 'And John Ashton?' she asked.

'There's a wife,' Faith answered, passing across the relevant file.

Liz opened it. 'Richmond, Surrey.' she read out loud. 'I'll go and see her. What do we tell them, Faith?'

'The minimum. That their husband or son was killed in action; that since they were working for Intelligence we can divulge no details. There may be special requests – if so, they'll be on file.'

Faith's matter-of-fact tone startled Liz.

'How many times have you had to do this?' she asked.

'Too many,' Faith answered. 'And it doesn't get any easier.'

Liz rose. 'Oh well,' she said, 'wish me luck.'

Faith smiled and picked up a pile of papers from the desk.

'And now,' she said grimly, 'we have to start looking for the next lot.'

As Liz left, Faith glanced at the sheet of paper on top of her pile. A small passport photo was clipped to it and a pretty dark-haired girl gazed back at her. God, how young she looks, thought Faith. She read the name of the applicant: Emily Whitbread.

Emily Whitbread was wearing her WAAF uniform.

'Do I look all right?' she asked.

'You look better than all right!' declared Miles.

'Oh, Miles!' she laughed.

'In fact, we make a jolly attractive couple,' he said, flicking imaginary dirt from the lapel of his RAF uniform.

Emily laughed, embarrassed as she always was when Miles tried to turn the two of them into a couple.

'Parkgrove Mansions,' she said, halting. 'This must be it.'

'I'll come and wait for you,' he said.

'You don't have to, Miles.'

'I didn't have to take my leave this week either,' he pointed out.

A couple of senior officers passed and Emily and Miles saluted.

'How long will you be?' Miles asked.

'I don't know! Could be slung out in five minutes!' said Emily lightly.

She was much more nervous than she could possibly have let on, even to Miles. Her education in a strict convent boarding-school had taught her to control her emotions and to mask her feelings.

'I hope you *are*,' said Miles seriously.

'Oh, that's very nice!' Emily felt aggrieved. He was always being condescending about her desire to see active service.

'Well, God, you don't think I want you going out there, do you?' he demanded.

Emily sighed. How could she make Miles understand about . . . well, everything?

Emily said a quick prayer outside the interview room, took a deep breath and then knocked tentatively. Inside, at the other end of a long table, there was an attractive red-haired woman in a smart suit.

'Please,' smiled the woman. 'Sit down.'

The first moments of the interview passed without a hitch, though Emily had a feeling that her voice sounded higher than usual. She confirmed that she had joined the WAAF straight from school; and yes, she had trained as a wireless operator.

Faith looked hard at Emily, thinking she looked even younger than in her passport photograph.

Emily looked nervously back. She thinks I'm too young, she thought, and of course I am. Far too inexperienced. What on earth am I doing here, wasting her time? There must be loads of . . .

'Sorry,' said Emily, realizing that the older woman had asked her a question, but not having a clue as to what it had been.

'How did you hear about our work?' asked Faith a second time. She smiled at the young candidate, to encourage her.

Emily relaxed a little.

'On the grapevine,' she replied. 'There was a rumour that pilots were dropping agents into France – women as well as men. I asked my CO about it and she was very cagey. But then I got your letter.'

'Why do you want to go out there?' Faith asked.

'I don't know,' Emily replied truthfully. 'I . . . just thought I might be useful.'

'Is that the only reason?' Faith probed.

'Isn't that enough? I mean, just wanting to help win the war?'

Faith made a small note on Emily's application form: PLUCK. She might have written NERVOUS or NAÏVE as well, or even instead; but she could not help liking this young applicant. Besides, Emily did have the necessary technical qualifications.

'We do badly need good operators in the field,' said Faith, pausing to study the look of relief which was crossing Emily's face.

'But,' she went on, 'being a good operator isn't the only requirement.

'I do speak French!' said Emily excitedly.

'How well?' Faith asked.

'I got a distinction in Matric – and I won the school prize for languages!'

Emily's voice trailed away as she saw the older woman looking at her sardonically. 'Two years running,' Emily added lamely.

'Have you been to France?'

'Oh, yes. Paris.'

'How long were you there?'

'Well . . .' Emily considered. 'Only three weeks. But our French teacher was a Parisienne, so I've had plenty of conversation practice.'

'All right, then let's talk in French for a bit,' And Faith rattled off a question about the political differences between various factions in the Resistance.

Emily felt all the confidence which had begun to accumulate rapidly disappearing. She couldn't understand a word that was being said to her. . .

*

John and Vivien Ashton's address in Richmond was a large, detached house. Trying to brace herself for the coming ordeal, Liz paused for a moment at the front gate before walking up the garden path.

The front door was opened by a striking woman in her forties. The brilliant red of the woman's lips and nail varnish took Liz aback, as did the boldness of her dress. A scarlet woman, she thought, before she could stop herself.

'Mrs Ashton?' Liz asked, hoping this was someone else.

'That's right,' answered the woman. Sure enough, she had a slightly 'off' accent.

'My name is Elizabeth Grainger. I work for the same organization as your husband did.'

Vivien Ashton laughed raucously.

'No! So it really does exist? I was beginning to . . .' Her voice trailed off as she realized the tense which Liz had used.

'*Did*?' asked Vivien softly.

The two women looked at each other. In that split second, Liz was aware that Vivien knew the reason for her visit.

'You'd better come in,' Vivien said.

The drawing-room surprised Liz with its taste and character. The room was crowded with paintings, prints and ornaments; obviously, Vivien was interested in the arts and especially in dance. Two exquisite models of ballet dancers stood on either side of the mirror hanging over the fireplace. In pride of place on the mantelpiece, however, was a silver-framed photo of John Ashton in uniform.

Vivien took a cigarette from a silver case which looked like those Cad always gave to his agents on leaving for

France. Vivien offered her visitor a cigarette and Liz accepted gratefully. The two women sat side by side on the sofa, as Liz went through her well-rehearsed speech.

'Poor old Johnny,' said Vivien slowly when Liz had come to a stop. For a time, Vivien sat staring down into her lap. The ash from her cigarette fell on to the floor.

'How did he cop it?' she asked finally.

'I'm afraid I can't tell you that,' Liz said gently.

Vivien shot her a hard look, full of hatred.

'The nature of his work demands absolute secrecy,' Liz explained, aware that she sounded priggish.

'Oh, yes,' said Vivien bitterly. 'Hush-bloody-hush!'

'For what its worth,' said Liz, conscious of her clumsiness and trying not to talk down to the other woman, 'your husband was a very brave man. No one could have served his country better.'

'For Christ's sake, spare me the clichés!' snapped Vivien.

'In this case, they happen to be true,' Liz retorted.

It's no good, she thought. I don't like Vivien Ashton, even though I feel sorry for her. Oh dear, I'm not doing this very well. The bereaved woman stared vacantly ahead of her into the fireplace, where a copper coal-scuttle was filled with what Liz considered an over-elaborate arrangement of bronze chrysanthemums.

'Is there anyone I can contact for you?' asked Liz.

Vivien paused, then slowly shook her head.

'You've no children?'

Again Vivien waited for a moment before replying. 'No, no family at all. Johnny's parents are dead as well as mine. Thank God!'

Liz wondered what Vivien meant and noticing Liz's curious look, Vivien explained.

'That must be the worst thing of all,' said Vivien, 'seeing your own child die before you.'

Into Liz's mind's eye flashed a picture of her own daughter, Vicky, swinging on the farm-gate near her mother's house down in Devon. Liz said that she agreed: she couldn't think of anything worse. For a moment, there was a kind of bond between the two of them.

'Presumably, he'll be buried wherever it happened,' Vivien stated rather than asked.

'Yes. After the war it may be possible to arrange for his remai . . .' Liz floundered for a moment. 'For him to be recovered.'

A brittle laugh came from Vivien.

'You make him sound like a stray parcel.'

Liz felt herself go schoolgirl-red with embarrassment. She was making a real hash of this.

'I'm sorry,' she murmured, genuinely upset by her own ineptitude.

'Anyway, Johnny wouldn't give a damn one way or the other. He was more interested in the quality of life than where his corpse rotted,' said Vivien.

Her smartly manicured fingers stubbed out yet another cigarette in the large onyx ashtray at her side. Meanwhile Liz consulted her papers, in an effort to turn the conversation to less emotional matters.

'He made a will before he left,' she said. 'It's lodged with your solicitors, Wilcocks and Bull.'

Cock and Bull, Johnny used to call them.' Vivien let out another harsh laugh and then stopped abruptly. She reached out for the silver case and lit another cigarette.

'I know how you must be feeling,' Liz ventured.

'Oh yes?' Vivien sneered.

'My brother was shot down over Germany,' Liz said quietly.

Vivien blew a smoke-ring, then turned and appraised Liz for the first time. She did not like her visitor; an English rose with a touch of frostbite had been her first assessment, and she saw no reason to alter that view. But now, at least, the woman was making an effort to be friendly.

'Boy, I wouldn't have your job!' she exclaimed. 'Is this what you do all day? Traipse round breaking the news to people?'

Liz felt herself colouring again. Apart from the very natural strain of the task in hand, she was rattled by the hostility she felt emanating from Vivien.

'Actually it's my first time,' she tried to excuse herself, 'which is why I'm making such a damn awful job of it.'

Vivien smiled, thought for a moment, then rose from the sofa and walked across the room to a chrome and glass cocktail cabinet. Vulgar, thought Liz, but expensive.

Vivien looked across at Liz. Stuck-up, she thought, but means well.

'I don't know about you,' said Vivien, 'but I could do with a snifter.

Emily pulled herself together and started to talk to Faith in French. At first she spoke haltingly, then she began to pick up speed.

Faith smiled at her. 'Well, your French is quite good,' she said.

Emily looked at her with relief.

'Oh . . . thank you,' she stammered.

'But,' Faith went on,' 'I'm afraid you'd never pass out there.'

Emily's smile disappeared.

'You've a pronounced English accent.'

Emily wasn't going to be put off that easily. She knew what she wanted to do. Knew also that one of her chief virtues was persistence. You need that, if you're going to survive in a family of seven children.

'Isn't that part of the training?' asked Emily. 'Brushing up our accents?'

'Yours needs rather more than brushing up,' Faith explained.

Emily leaned forward in her chair and looked at Faith with great self-assurance. 'I'm sure I could do it with practice. I've a good ear and . . .'

But before she could continue, Faith cut in.

'Emily, we're not talking about getting through Matric. Out there you'd have to pass as a native. Not just with the Germans – you might get by with them – but with the French people themselves. Not all of them would be your friends, you know.'

'I *could* do it. I *know* I could!' Emily said, almost petulantly. 'I just know I could, if you give me a chance!'

BRAVE, PERSISTENT, wrote Faith, followed by the word WHY? She underlined this last word a couple of times, then looked again at the young girl who shifted anxiously in her chair.

'What about your commitments?' asked Faith.

'How do you mean?' responded Emily.

'Are your parents alive?' elucidated Faith.

'Oh, yes. My father's a doctor in Somerset.'

'Have you a fiancé or boyfriend?'

'I've a boyfriend; he's in the RAF. But we're not engaged,' Emily added rather too hastily.

'How would you feel about leaving him?'

'Men are leaving their girlfriends all the time.' She looked straight at Faith. 'He'd just have to lump it.'

'You're a Catholic?' Faith looked at the application form.

'Yes.'

'Practising?'

'Yes. But not about to take holy orders or anything.'

'You realize that if you were selected you'd have to lie to your parents?'

Emily considered this for a moment.

'Yes,' she said thoughtfully. 'But they probably won't ask me much.'

Faith looked at her quizzically.

'I've two brothers and four sisters, and now they've got evacuees too. They tend to lose track,' Emily explained lightly. 'Probably they won't even notice.'

Faith underlined the word WHY? again. Well, she thought, Emily doesn't believe in expressing her feelings. And in many ways that's all to the good. A shame about the accent, though.

'Thank you,' said Faith, rising to her feet to bring the interview to an end.

'When will I hear?' asked Emily, also standing.

'I beg your pardon?'

'If I've been accepted, I mean. When will I hear?'

'By the end of the week,' replied Faith, amused at her forthrightness. 'It's all right. We don't believe in keeping you in suspense for long.'

Emily left the room, unsure how she had performed but relieved that at least she hadn't been rejected on the spot. She found Miles waiting for her in the Parkgrove library; he was sitting in one of the overstuffed leather armchairs, apparently engrossed in the newspaper. His interest in her interview seemed less than intense; but perhaps, thought Emily, he wants to wait until we're alone before finding out how I got on.

'Shall we go and have a cup of tea?' she suggested.

'I've a better idea,' said Miles casually. 'We'll go to my brother's flat.'

Emily shot him a sideways look.

'He's away,' Miles explained. 'Didn't I tell you?'

Liz had drunk rather more gin than she intended at Vivien's, and left the Richmond house feeling less hostile towards her. She had even given Vivien her direct telephone number, in case she needed any help. Probably the woman would never use it; she seemed very self-sufficient.

The journey from Richmond to Knightsbridge passed quickly, and Liz had quite forgotten the time as she opened the front door of her mansion flat. The radio was on, with some kind of educational talk droning out. Laurence must have got home before her; she called out to him as she shut the door behind her.

He emerged from the kitchen – hot, sweaty and bad-tempered. He was in uniform, but had taken off his jacket. Liz pecked him on one flushed cheek, removed her coat and hung it on the coat-stand by the front door. Then she followed Laurence into the kitchen, taking the pins out of her hat.

'I've started supper,' said Laurence pointedly. 'It was the stew, I take it?'

'Yes,' Liz nodded. 'Well done.'

She decided to jolly him along by asking about his day.

'Mostly paperwork – for the court-martial,' he said. 'And yours? More talks to trainees?'

'I had to tell a woman that her husband had been killed.'

'One of your agents?'

'Yes. Although she doesn't know that, of course.'

Laurence gazed thoughtfully at Liz. 'That could have been me,' he said.

'What?'

'Could have been that Ashley woman coming to tell me you'd been killed. God, when I look back! You must have been mad!'

Liz closed her eyes briefly, making herself bite back the anger she felt whenever Laurence spoke dismissively about the Outfit. Turning on her heels, she walked out of the kitchen, down the corridor and into the bedroom; she needed a few minutes on her own to calm down. She couldn't remember how many times Laurence had blamed her for joining the Outfit, and especially for going to France. Much as he might wish it, their marriage could never return to its old pattern.

Sitting at her dressing-table, Liz attacked her ash-blonde hair vigorously with sharp strokes of her hair-brush. The innocent gaze of five-year-old Vicky stared out almost reproachfully at her from a picture frame as she continued brushing. She felt defiant. It wasn't possible to turn back the clock. Laurence and her mother, Evelyn, would have to come to terms with the fact that active service had changed her. She had survived . . . she was her own person.

Her eyes passed from the photograph to the silver compact lying on the dressing-table. Opening the case, she re-read for the thousandth time the inscription which Cad engraved for every one of his agents: *Bonne Chance*. Her mind wandered back to her time in France, and especially her last brief interlude with Kit. There had been real passion there, thought Liz: not just a fling given added spice by their proximity to danger. For Kit, she had known an intensity of feeling that she had never experienced with Laurence. Poor Laurence, she thought guiltily. She wondered how Kit was faring . . . It was over a year since he had been dropped in Area 3.

She was brought out of her reverie by Laurence, announcing sharply that dinner was ready. Liz laid the hairbrush down on the dressing-table and made a big effort to push all thoughts of Kit from her mind.

While Miles struggled with her blouse, Emily struggled with her conscience. He was having great difficulty with the buttons; he seemed to weigh a ton, and his brother's sofa was far from comfortable. Although he had attempted to create the right atmosphere by putting a record of one of Tchaikovsky's string serenades on the gramophone, Emily still felt hot and bothered, torn between sense and sensuality.

Miles pulled away from her. Feeling his eyes on her body, she smiled adoringly back at him, although she knew her hair was dishevelled and she must look a mess. His hand travelled up her thigh, under her skirt, and she sat up abruptly.

'No, Miles! Please! You promised!' she gasped.

Miles's boyish, handsome face twisted with disappointment. 'I know, but . . .' he pouted.

Emily rapidly fastened her blouse and sat on the edge of the sofa with her hands wrapped round her knees. She rocked backwards and forwards, feeling confused, miserable and guilty.

'I said we shouldn't come back here.'

'You want it, don't you?' asked Miles, his voice sharp with frustration.

'Yes,' said Emily. And it was true. 'But . . .'

'I'd be careful,' he promised, tapping his pocket.

'It's not just that,' she replied, shaking her head. 'It's just, I'd rather . . .'

'Wait until you're married,' said Miles in a long-suffering voice.

'I know it sounds—'

'But you won't even get engaged!' Miles was exasperated. 'Come on, Em! You could be off on some damn course in a week or two, and then God knows when we'll see each other again.'

Emily stood up. 'I'm sorry,' she said, looking tenderly down at him.

'I wouldn't lose respect for you,' he told her.

Emily pulled at her skirt to straighten it.

'But I might for myself,' she said softly.

Miles leaned back in the sofa and shook his head.

'Why the hell,' he groaned, 'did I have to pick a virgin?'

When Faith returned to the office from her interviewing, she was surprised to find Cad about to leave. On most days he worked late into the evening, all thought of family life pushed to one side.

'So how are we doing?' he asked, pulling on his raincoat.

'I've found six, and I'm not sure about a seventh.'

Cad put on his cap and looked at her curiously.

'Emily Whitbread,' Faith explained. 'The WAAF who applied off her own bat.'

'What's she like?'

'Very young and very determined. Of course, the fact that she's already an experienced wireless operator is a terrific bonus.'

Cad looked at Faith shrewdly. 'So what are your reservations?'

'Her French. It'll need a lot of work.'

'Then see she gets it,' said Cad decisively. 'You know how desperate we are for operators.'

He touched his cap and departed, leaving Faith to reflect that this would be the first time Cad would get home in time for dinner for several weeks. Some domestic crisis must be brewing.

The following day, the atmosphere of quiet concentration in Liz's and Faith's office was disturbed by the arrival of Ned. In his capacity as propaganda officer, he supplied Faith with false messages to be transmitted by the BBC later that evening. Instead of leaving, however, he lounged against the office door and nonchalantly blew smoke rings up at the ceiling.

Ned always managed to rile Liz. It wasn't just his frivolous attitude which annoyed her, but his perpetual questions about life out in the field – and in particular his prying about Kit, or her 'brother in arms' as he called him. She understood that Ned was desperately jealous of Kit's practical experience, and indeed her own; but still she found him exasperating.

'You know, I'm surprised he hasn't cracked up,' remarked Ned.

'Who?' Liz asked.

'Kit, of course,' he said.

Faith looked up from her paper-work. She could sense the atmosphere between her two colleagues.

'Well, he's never asked to come back,' said Faith.

Ned laughed. 'Perhaps he's got a bit of French crackling hidden away!'

'Oh, for heaven's sake!' Liz snapped.

'Strikes me the only way they get themselves replaced these days is by being shot,' Ned said cheerily as he left the room.

Liz threw down the newspapers she had been working on.

'Why must he always be so damn flippant?' she complained.

Faith knew that Liz was sensitive on the subject of Kit, and reassured her that he should soon be safely back in Britain.

'Cad is looking for a replacement, Liz,' she said sympathetically.

Liz gave her a quick look. Sometimes she wondered how much Faith really knew about Kit and herself. Perhaps it would help for her to unload her feelings about Kit on to Faith's sympathetic shoulders? Perhaps this was the moment to do so . . . or perhaps not. Suddenly, there was a phone call on Liz's special line. It was Vivien Ashton, asking to see her.

Even at a distance, Vivien was an unmistakable sight on the tow-path at Richmond, a striking figure much brighter than the grey summer day. She wore a flamboyant hat and matching coat. As she turned in greeting and held out a gloved hand, Liz wondered why she was not wearing black.

'Thanks for coming.'

'I told you,' said Liz, 'if there's anything I can do to help. . . .'

The two women walked side by side along the river bank.

'There is.' Vivien was evidently a woman who believed

in coming straight to the point. 'I want you to fix up for me to see the big white chief.'

Liz looked at her in surprise.

'Colonel James Cadogan,' Vivien continued. 'Head of the French Section of the Outfit. Or should I say the Organization for the Infiltration of Occupied Territories?'

She laughed as she saw Liz's expression of incredulity. 'There! That took you by surprise, didn't it?' she said boastfully.

'How did you find out?' Liz asked softly.

'Johnny left a letter. Telling lies must have gone against the grain.'

'Why do you want to see Colonel Cadogan?'

'That's my business, isn't it? Tell him it's a dinner invitation.'

Liz did not like Vivien any more than she had done at first, but she did feel a certain admiration for the woman's gall.

'I'll pass on your message,' she promised, 'but I really can't guarantee anything.'

'Why aren't you in uniform?' asked Vivien, as she took Cad's coat from him and hung it up. He was wearing an extremely well-cut grey lounge suit.

'Outside the office, I only wear it on official business. Otherwise I prefer to . . .'

'Remain anonymous.' completed Vivien with a smile.

'And comfortable,' Cad added.

Attractive woman, he thought. But rather a loud get-up. It reminded him of something one might have seen in a theatrical production before the war. Hardly widow's weeds.

'I suppose you're wondering why I'm not in mourning?' asked Vivien, aware of a slightly disapproving expression on Cad's face. 'Johnny hated that sort of thing.'

'I'm so sorry about John.' said Cad. 'I regarded him as a friend as well as a valued agent. I knew him before the war.'

'Yes,' Vivien nodded. 'Your name rang a bell. We used to supply you with wine, didn't we?'

She poured Cad a large whisky as he looked round the drawing room. A dining-table in the bay window at the end of the room, overlooking the garden, was laid for two.

'Is that how you came to recruit him?' asked Vivien, handing him his drink.

'He was an obvious candidate with his knowledge of France.'

'We met out there, you know. I was an actress – of sorts. Cabaret and that. I was doing a season in "Gay Paree".'

Cad raised his glass and together they toasted 'Gay Paree'. He couldn't help smiling as Vivien lit the candles on the dining-table.

'What's the joke?' she asked.

'Nothing,' said Cad, as they sat down.

'Are you worried that I might be trying to seduce you?' asked Vivien.

'Of course not,' lied Cad, who had been thinking precisely that.

'Well, in a way I am.'

Cad spluttered on his whisky.

'You see,' said Vivien, 'I want to join the Outfit.'

Up to now, she explained, her contribution to the war effort had been working for the NAAFI, going round the big estates and buying up cellars on the cheap.

As they ate, Cad wondered whether some of the extremely good Pol Roger '29 with which she was plying him had come via an aristocratic cellar. Not that he was complaining. Such luxuries were to be relished on the few occasions when they were available. The meal was also superb; Vivien had certainly put on quite a display for his benefit, and had used up many coupons to provide a splendid feast.

One by one, Vivien countered Cad's objections to her becoming an agent. It wasn't her age; Cad denied that it was her sex.

She was surprised to learn that Liz had worked in the field. 'I'd have thought she'd be much too refined for that sort of thing.'

'You'd be surprised,' Cad told her.

'So,' said Vivien, refilling his glass once again, 'if it's not my age or sex, what have you got against me?'

Cad sipped his champagne for a moment.

'Apart from anything else, it's less than a week since you heard about John. You haven't had time to get used to the—'

She cut in before he could finish his sentence.

'I don't need time,' she insisted.

'Of course you do. You're still in a state of shock. It's far too soon—'

Vivien interrupted again.

'All right! I'm cut up about Johnny. Well, Christ, we were married for twenty years! But this isn't some sort of hysterical reaction.'

Cad looked at her carefully and Vivien coolly returned his gaze.

'I'm not the hysterical sort,' she said emphatically.

'Look . . . Vivien,' Cad said wearily, 'an agent requires all sorts of skills and qualities that—'

'Johnny was good enough for you,' she protested.

'Yes, but—'

'So what assets did he have that I haven't got? Or would have, with training? I speak French as well as he did. Better! I was the one who dealt with the vineyard owners.'

Cad tried not to show a stirring of interest at hearing this.

'I've got all his know-how,' Vivien continued, 'and more. I might not be Sarah Bernhardt, but I could pass myself off as most things. Then there are my drawings too. Wouldn't that be useful? Sketches of buildings and that? I tell you, Cad, you'd be mad to turn me down.'

Loud bursts of opera issued forth from a long open-topped Lagonda as it sped its way through the twisting lanes of the English countryside. Vivien loved singing and she also loved driving fast. She even loved her new uniform. With a screech of tyres she braked to negotiate an unexpectedly sharp bend, and almost ran over a small figure also wearing a FANY uniform and carrying a rather battered suitcase. Slamming the brakes on, Vivien halted and reversed at high speed towards Emily, who was looking with some wonderment at the exotic car and equally striking driver.

She leaned out and asked Emily if she was also going to Ettingley Manor. When she said she was, Vivien told her to hop in. Emily accepted the offer of a lift with alacrity. The walk from the station was proving much longer than she had thought and her case, which had seemed light when she started off, now seemed to be packed with lead. She shoved the suitcase into the back of the car and got in next to Vivien.

'Do you work there?' asked Vivien, putting the car into gear and driving off, 'or are you going on this course?'

Emily looked suspiciously at her driver. Was this some trick that the Outfit were playing. She was aware that she had been a borderline selection, and wanted to do nothing that would prejudice her final assessment.

'Er . . . what course would that be?' She asked innocently.'

'Vivien laughed and slapped the driving-wheel with her hands in merriment.

'Oh, I see you're going to make a splendid agent!'

'Sorry, I thought you might be testing me,' apologized Emily, not wanting to seem stand-offish.

Vivien liked the look of this pretty young girl and gave her one of her most engaging smiles.

'Righto, let's start as we mean to go on.' Vivien introduced herself. 'I'm Solange. Who are you?'

Emily also introduced herself by her code name, which was Zoe.

They fell into easy conversation as Vivien drove wildly through the countryside. Emily warmed to the slightly eccentric older woman and her feelings of apprehension began to diminish.

However, even Vivien was silenced by the approach to Ettingley Manor. The long gravel drive was flanked and overhung by gloomy rhododendrons. Then the building – a vast grey Gothic pile – loomed into view, and looked even more forbidding.

'You wouldn't think this was Surrey,' said Vivien, finally screeching to a stop. 'Looks more like Transylvania!'

The recruits were a mixture of military and civilian, men

and women, and from all classes of society. There were five women on the course; but as the training progressed, the quiet Emily and the flamboyant Vivien stuck together and became close friends.

The month at Ettingley was spent in intensive training. The would-be agents were taught how to survive in the wild, self-defence, how to use explosives and handle guns, how to shin up drainpipes and enter rooms undetected, how to pick locks with a hairpin. In areas where the traineees were weak, they were given extra tuition. Emily spent as much time as possible bringing her French up to scratch, practising her conversation with Vivien and a newly-arrived French recruit.

One evening after a hard day spent exercising out in the fields, followed by a long lecture given by Liz, Vivien and Emily were resting in their dormitory. Emily lay sprawled on her bed, reading a book; Vivien had had enough studying for one day and was painting her nails which had been chipped by the day's exertions.

Emily pushed her dark hair out of her eyes and put her book face down open on the bed to keep her place. She leaned across towards the older woman and confided her worries about the initiative test which they were all being given the next day.

'I wonder what the worst thing will be?' she said.

Vivien stretched her nails out in front of her to admire her handiwork. 'Crossing a pool of sulphuric acid,' she said casually.

Emily's face fell in dismay. 'Moses!' she exclaimed dismally.

'Nothing to it,' Vivien continued, in her nonchalant fashion. 'You just make stepping-stones across. You'll find some blocks of wood in the undergrowth.'

Emily looked at her new-found friend with astonishment.

'How do you know?'

This time it was Vivien's turn to confide.

'As a matter of fact, I eavesdropped on a couple of chaps who did it yesterday.'

For a moment, Emily looked shocked. 'Isn't that cheating?' she exclaimed.

'What do you think this is?' said Vivien. 'The Girl Guides?'

As Emily realized her own naïvety, she joined in with Vivien's hoots of laughter.

Towards the end of the month, each recruit had to undergo a psychiatric interview. As Vivien came out of hers with a wicked smile on her face, Emily and a young male trainee were sitting waiting for their turn; they had been nervously flicking through French magazines, but could not really concentrate on them.

Vivien came up behind the pair and tapped the young man on his shoulder.

'OK, Pierre, your turn for the couch,' she said.

'What's he like?' asked Pierre, getting up.

'Like all psychiatrists – mad as a hatter,' Vivien laughed. Don't forget to tell him your Exotic Sheik Fantasy!'

'What did you have to do?' asked Emily anxiously.

Vivien sat down next to her friend.

'Stare at a lot of blots first. Then he asks you what they look like.'

'What *do* they look like?'

'Blots. Only you don't say that. You say spiders and Churchill and suet pud.'

Emily looked perplexed as Vivien continued.

'Then he'll ask you a load of damn-fool questions about

your parents. My God, if I'd told him the truth he'd have had a field day! And *you* be careful what answers you give, Zoe. Tell him you're one of seven children and he'll think you're only doing this through a subconscious desire to be noticed.'

'Perhaps I am,' muttered Emily.

'So bally what? What does it matter why we want to go, so long as we do? We all have our reasons.'

There was something about the way Vivien spoke that caused Emily to glance at her friend thoughtfully.

With Laurence away out of town on a case, Liz and Faith spent a 'girls only' evening together in the Knightsbridge flat. The two of them had a thoroughly pleasant and relaxing time. Liz's mother, Evelyn, had sent some food up from the country and they had quite a feast. The table had been cleared and the dishes washed up, when they settled down for a cup of ersatz coffee.

Liz lay back on the sofa with her legs up while Faith lounged in Laurence's high-backed armchair, reading a letter home from Vicky. It was full of complaints about school food and the wonders of someone called Primrose Weatherby.

Faith refolded the letter and placed it back in its envelope. 'Jolly good handwriting,' she told Liz, passing back the letter.

Faith was secretly rather moved by the innocent scrawl. Although previously married, she had divorced years ago without having any children. Now she lived in a small flat with her sister, who had no idea what her real work involved.

There were times when Faith felt that the Outfit's

trainees had taken the place of the children she might have had. She looked across at Liz. They were certainly closer to each other than mere work colleagues. Not so much mother and daughter, either: more like sisters.

Liz tucked the precious envelope back into her handbag and laughed.

'Even if the spelling leaves a bit to be desired!' she said, proud nevertheless of Vicky's progress.

Liz resumed her position lying on the sofa and her thoughts started to wander.

'This time last year,' she mused aloud, 'little did I think she'd be dug in at a boarding-school and I'd be . . . what am I?'

Suddenly her voice took on an unaccustomed edge. 'An ex-secret agent,' she answered herself.

Faith looked at Liz over the top of her spectacles.

'You do miss it, don't you?' she asked, quietly probing.

'It's ridiculous, I know. Half the time I was scared out of my wits. And yet when Matty went back into the field . . . I almost envied her.'

'The work you're doing now is essential too, Liz.'

'I know, but it's not like *being* there,' Liz murmured.

'You'll settle down.'

'Will I? Perhaps you could tell me *how*. That's one thing the Outfit doesn't teach us. You train us, change us, send us out . . . then bring us home and expect us to pick up our lives as if nothing had ever happened.'

The next day Faith and Liz met again, this time to discuss with Cad the current crop of recruits. To his great regret. they had to turn down one of the best male trainees because he talked in his sleep, which would leave him wide open as a security risk. Cad indulged in one of his customary bursts of spleen against the Gaullists, before going on to consider the women.

Faith looked down at Emily's report. It was very good; she had passed everything except shooting with flying colours. Cad questioned her competence with French.

'She's worked like a Trojan,' said Faith. 'There's still the trace of an English accent, but if we give her a colonial background . . . that covers a multitude of sins.'

Cad nodded. 'I'll leave that with you, Wireless operator,' he noted down. 'Next?'

'Peter Slade. "Antoine". Major Duncan recommends we send him on the Leader's course.'

'Good,' said Cad. 'That's what I had hoped. I've got him pencilled in to replace Kit Vanston. Any more, Liz?'

The knowledge that Kit was finally returning home plunged Liz deep into thought. Cad had to repeat his question before she realized what was going on and looked up with a start.'

'Sorry,' she apologized. 'Yes. "Solange". Vivien Ashton.'

'Ah, yes,' said Cad.

'She appears to have broken every rule in the book, and led the psychiatrist a merry dance too. Both he and Major Duncan rate her highly; they say she's resourceful, intelligent, strongly motivated.'

'But you don't like her,' commented Cad perceptively.

'Not much, but that doesn't come into it,' said Liz, trying to be fair. No, she did not much like Vivien. She thought back to the session she had had with the women recruits about personal matters. Asked by Emily about the curse, Liz had explained that periods might be a bit erratic, with the shock of everything, and had also warned her to take some rags as French STs were useless.

Vivien, of course, had had to be flippant about all that,

saying she would have no problems, having had a hysterectomy. What was of much more concern to her was the situation with regard to cosmetics.

Faith interrupted Liz's train of thought by expressing some doubts about Vivien as well.

'Odd that she didn't find herself some worthwhile work before. Something more edifying than keeping the NAAFI in wine.'

'And siphoning off crates for herself,' added Cad, remembering the dinner he had had at Vivien's house in Richmond.

'She probably needed a trigger, like I did,' put in Liz, who was desperately trying to be open-minded.

'Do you think she might make a team with Emily?' suggested Cad.

'They're certainly opposites,' said Liz, 'but they seem to get on well with each other.'

'Well,' said Cad, 'let's put them together and see how they get on in their initiative test. Find out how they operate in the field together.'

'Ah yes,' said the instructor. 'A nice little test for you two – I want you to steal a car.'

He saw the wink that Vivien gave to Emily, as if to say 'piece of cake', and frowned. He decided to emphasize the difficulty of the project.

'It's a chauffeur-driven Bentley and it belongs to the Chief Constable of the county. Have it back here by dark.'

Emily and Vivien grimaced at each other.

The pair of them cycled over to the Chief Constable's house and reconnoitred. Crouching behind the hedge which surrounded the imposing house, they watched as a man with rolled-up sleeves polished a gleaming black Bentley parked in the gravel drive.

Vivien lowered her binoculars and whispered to Emily. 'That looks like the chauffeur. Can't see his nibs cleaning the car, can you?'

Emily took the binoculars and frowned.

'Well,' said Vivien. 'No time to waste. You'd better go and make up to him.'

Emily looked at her companion curiously.

'Find out when he'll be driving his boss to work,' Vivien explained.

'Wouldn't you be better at that?' asked Emily, who suddenly felt rather nervous.

'He mustn't see me; my star performance comes later. Go on, just roll those big baby eyes.'

Emily rose from her crouching position, pulled her skirt straight and set off towards the house, coughing apologetically to attract the chauffeur's attention as she approached him.

'Excuse me – I'm sorry to trouble you, but I seem to be lost.' She smiled her most winning smile.

Having elicited the necessary information, Emily rejoined Vivien and the pair set off to lie in wait for the Chief Constable's car. They positioned themselves on either side of a crossroads not far from the house; when Emily saw the Bentley travelling down the lane in their direction, she signalled to Vivien.

Vivien clambered on to her bicycle and set off towards the crossroads. As the car turned the corner and drove towards her, she swerved. Dramatically, she threw herself in front of the oncoming car. The Bentley pulled up with a screech and the chauffeur leapt out, leaving his door wide open. Meanwhile Emily made her way round to the back of the vehicle and crouched. The Chief

Constable also got out of the back seat and went across to inspect the scene of the 'accident'.

Vivien was doing her drama queen act for all that it was worth. Having positioned herself carefully, so that the two men couldn't see Emily creeping up on the car, with a gesture like the dying swan Vivien flung herself into the arms of the Chief Constable – and Emily seized her chance, darting round the side of the Bentley and climbing into the driver's seat.

Vivien would always remember the look of astonishment on the faces of the two men as the car roared past and disappeared down the road.

Although she was desperate to know, Liz carefully chose the time when she asked Faith about Cad's plans for Kit. She was not sure how much the other woman knew, and did not want to reveal too much about her own feelings for him. After all, she thought, as far as Faith is aware I'm a happily married woman.

The occasion arose as the two women went for a lunchtime stroll in Regent's Park. Respecting Liz's attempts to conceal the affair, Faith tried to look as if she imagined that the question was a completely disinterested one from a former colleague's of Kit's.

'A good long leave first, I imagine,' she replied.

'It'll be even more difficult for him than for me to acclimatize,' commented Liz. 'After all, he's been away so long.'

'And he's got to get used to more than just coming home. It'll be home without his wife and children.'

'Yes,' said Liz sadly.

There was a short silence, as they studied the pigeons.

'Has Cad decided on the new leader for Area 7?' asked Liz, changing the subject.

'No, not yet. He's waiting for the report on Zoe and Solange.'

A handsome figure cycled up to Parkgrove Mansions, dressed in naval uniform and whistling to himself. Colin was now very different from the callow trainee he had once been at Ettingley Manor, where he first met Matty and Liz. Now considerably more thoughtful and adult, he had just sailed through his Leaders' course and was itching to get back to France.

Cad noticed the difference in Colin's attitude with approval as the two of them sat hunched over a map of France. They were sitting in squashy armchairs in a corner of what must once have been one of the hotel's grandest reception rooms.

Cad indicated to Colin the area that he wanted to send him to. Area 7 was down in the south-west part of France and extended all the way into the foothills leading up into the Pyrenees.

'Well away from your previous stamping ground,' commented Cad. 'You'd be centred here in Montaud.' He pointed on the map to a small town to the west of Toulouse.

'It's become one of our key areas since they occupied the South,' Cad continued. 'The previous team did quite a bit of ground-work, but since they were caught we've only just kept communications going.'

Colin wanted to know about the local resistance.

'Very fragmented,' said Cad. 'Various local groups. Communists. Free French – for as much as that's worth!'

Colin suppressed a smile. Cad always had to have his obligatory dig at de Gaulle's lot.

'And,' Cad concluded, 'there's a section of the Maquis hiding up here in the Pyrenees.'

Colin studied the map and then looked at Cad.

'And my job would be to coordinate them?'

'Coordinate them, train them, knock them into shape. As you may have guessed, the Allies are planning to invade France in the not-too-distant future. A lot will depend on the back-up we can give them from within.'

'I'll do my best,' Colin assured Cad.

'We'll find you a water-tight cover story to account for your exemption from forced labour.'

'Who else will be in my team?'

'I'm going to transfer a sabotage chap from Area 6. Gaspard, one of our best; he'll contact you out there. The other two are women.'

For one moment Colin thought it might be the old team of Liz and Matty, and his eyes lit up. He had respect for Liz and still carried a torch for Matty.

'No, she's busy elsewhere now,' Cad told him, reading his thoughts. 'But the pair you're getting are good. You'll be meeting them on the parachute course.'

The next few days were passed in frenetic activity. Emily, Vivien and Colin underwent parachute training, as Faith and Liz made preparations for the group's departure to France.

It was during periods like this that Liz realized fully how calmly efficient Faith was. Despite the importance that Churchill laid on the Outfit's work with his instructions to make Europe burn. Cad and Faith had very little real authority. Most of Faith's time seemed to be spent in trying to wheedle facilities and equipment from the regular Forces.

'Got it!' cried Faith one day.

'What?' asked Liz.

'The plane to fly Colin's team to France,'

'At last!' congratulated Liz. 'How did you do it?'

'I had to be extremely charming to an awful lot of people,' explained Faith. 'I'm not surprised that Cad sometimes gets depressed.'

'When can they go?' Liz asked.

'Send a message to France,' said Faith, 'that a team will be on their way at the next full moon.'

Louis brought the message to Marie and as soon as he left Leon Ferrier's shop, she began to close up. To her dismay she was interrupted by her neighbour, Annette, who was standing just outside. The woman was a widow, obviously lonely and one of the town's greatest gossips. She intensely irritated Marie with her incessant prying; but, being a good-natured woman, Marie always passed the time of day with her.

'He's in quite a lot, isn't he?' Annette enquired.

'Thank goodness someone is,' Marie replied.

She went back into the room behind the shop, where Leon worked and slept. In a corner was a small metal bed and along one wall was his work-bench piled with articles waiting to be repaired or ready for collection. He was repairing a radio as Marie came in.

'Louis?' he asked, turning the wheels of his wheelchair so that he could look directly at Marie.

She nodded.

'What did he want?' Leon asked tetchily.

Marie rubbed her hands on her overall. 'The British are sending in another team. He wants us to house the wireless operator.'

Leon shook his head. 'It's far too risky,' he said.

'Look what *they're* risking,' pleaded Marie.

'It's one thing passing on messages and doing the odd repair, but having a "pianist" under our roof! There'd be a detector van round here in no time!'

'She won't be transmitting from here. It's just a base she needs.'

'Why us? There are other people with more space!'

'They know they can trust us.'

'Us, maybe, but there are others in the street. Look at that blabbermouth opposite.'

'Annette is harmless enough.' Marie persisted in her argument. 'Louis thinks that the Allies are hoping to mount an invasion by the end of the year. They'll need all the help we can give them.' She looked hard at her father. 'Don't you want to be free of the Boche?' she demanded.

'God in heaven! You say that to *me* ?' He hit his useless legs frustratedly. 'Do you think I wouldn't shoot every last one of them if I had a chance?'

'She could sleep in the store-room,' Marie continued.

Now it was Leon's turn to look hard at Marie.

'It's Luc I'm thinking of,' said Leon quietly. 'You've already lost a husband. Do you want to lose your son?'

Marie looked at him in dismay.

'A stranger arriving here? It'll only attract attention. They'd check our papers like as not, as well as Luc's, and be bound to notice he's coming up for twenty. Next thing, they'll be dragging him off to some god-forsaken camp in Germany, like Simone's boy.'

'It's all right, grandad.'

The words came from a tall thin, tousled figure who had been standing in the back doorway listening to the heated conversation. The lad stood twisting a bicycle wheel in his hand.

'You needn't worry about me,' said Luc. 'I shan't be here.' He turned to face his mother. 'I was going to tell you later. I've decided to join the Maquis.'

Faith was amused at the vigour with which Emily played the piano. All the other recruits were joining in the celebration at the end of the parachute training course and the Officers' Mess at Ringway shook to their own version of the 'Hokey Cokey'. Colin and Vivien led the dancing round the edge of the room.

You press your *feet* and knees
You tuck your *elbow* in.
You force your head right down
Till you've got a double chin,
You do the Hokey Cokey
And you're para-chu-*tin'*
And that's what it's all about!

Faith stood at the edge of the dance floor, having come up specially for the party. She laughed with pleasure at the sight of the young men and women so determined to enjoy themselves.

'They're like a lot of children,' she commented to Phil, the Lancastrian instructor who had put the recruits through their parachuting paces.

He chuckled. 'At least they're doing it *here*. Remember that crowd who took weekend leave and ended up doing parachute rolls on the dance floor at the Astor?'

'And Cad complains about Free French security,' Faith said wryly.

The 'Hokey Cokey' ended and the dancers drifted off to the bar. Emily started playing some quieter tunes.

Colin bought Vivien a large drink and they touched glasses.

'Break a leg,' said Vivien. 'Did you do any musicals when you were acting?'

'How did you know I was an actor?'

'Aha! I dug out my old theatre programmes. I saw you in *Candida*.'

Colin grinned. 'Fame at last!'

'You were good.' Vivien had always remembered the handsome actor.

'I knew we'd get on well,' said Colin, who felt at ease with Vivien. 'Who else have you sniffed out?'

'Most of them. A right old hotch-potch.'

They looked round the room and Vivien pointed out each one by turn. There was a miner, a film stunt-man, a garage mechanic, a dress designer. Finally their eyes came to rest on Emily, who was immersed in her piano playing.

'And Zoe's a nice little Girl Guide who's far too naïve to be going on this caper,' concluded Vivien.

They don't think so,' asserted Colin.

'They only see what they want to see, and they need good wireless operators.

'What do you see?' Colin asked.

'Myself at that age,' replied Vivien ruefully. 'Come on, let's have a sing-song.'

She walked over to the piano.

'Here, Zoe!' she called out. 'Play Gory Gory!'

Emily looked up, smiled and broke into the recruits' version of 'Glory Glory Hallelujah'.

'They're in good spirits!' remarked Phil to Faith. 'That's something.'

Faith's face clouded. 'I always think it's a kind of safety valve against what lies ahead.'

'France?'

'Or Ravensbruck,' said Faith grimly.

Now there were only days to go and Emily concentrated hard at the 'Finishing School'. Suddenly she knew – really knew – that her life would depend on everything she learned. Again and again she rehearsed her assumed identity and familiarized herself with the area into which they were being sent.

She was grateful that Liz seemed to take such a personal interest in her, helping to fit her with French clothes, made in the Outfit's own tailor's workshop in Margaret Street. French jackets were a good ten inches longer than English ones, and it was most important that all such details were correct. Liz even took Emily to have her hair done in a French style by a recently-arrived refugee.

Though worried about Emily's immaturity. Liz was impressed by the extent to which she had grown up during the month's training She might look young still, but she was now more confident of her own abilities.

Liz allowed Emily to interrogate her about her own personal experiences in France. On their last evening together, Emily seemed concerned to hear whether Liz had had to sleep with any Germans. Shaking her head, the older woman thought back sadly to her friend Claudine, who had compromised the whole circuit, and – looking across at Emily, so obviously still a virgin – wondered if she would die as one.

Liz went to Viven's home in Richmond for their final

session. Even now, there was a thinly disguised atmosphere of tension between them and Vivien scorned Liz's offer to write to anyone while she was away.

When Liz told her how she had had to put Vicky in boarding-school and arrange for postcards to be sent to her daughter each week, Vivien looked at Liz sympathetically.

'That why you chucked it in?' asked Vivien.

'I didn't chuck it in,' Liz retorted. 'They recalled me.'

'Why?' asked Vivien. 'If you were such a damn good agent?'

'It was Cad's decision,' said Liz, nettled. 'Well, Cad and Kit's, my leader.'

'With a child it *would* be difficult.'

'Then of course there was my husband. He put his foot down . . . or tried to.'

'Men taking all the decisions! I thought the war had finished that.'

For the first time, the women locked eyes and felt a common bond.

As the day of departure approached, Cad was annoyed to find that he had to spend more and more of his time in Whitehall. Churchill had chosen this moment to appoint the Outfit to coordinate all Resistance work, which meant that Cad was now virtually an absentee from Baker Street. Fortunately, both Faith and Liz were around to take over more of his work.

Cad usually liked to see his agents off on their way, but this time the night of the full moon was impossible; there was to be a high-level ministerial conference which he could not avoid attending.

He looked in on Faith and Liz. 'Stand in for me tonight,

would you, Faith?' he asked. 'Or would you rather meet Kit? We must give him an official reception.'

Faith shot a glance at Liz. 'Oh, I think Liz should do that,' she said.

The day before the flight, Emily had phoned Miles, who was on a course.

'Long time, no hear,' he said.

'Can I see you?'

'When?'

'Tonight.'

'It's a bit awkward.'

'It has to be tonight.'

'Oh. Well, I suppose I could wangle the evening off. Where shall we meet?'

'How about your brother's flat?'

There was a pause.

'Righto.'

Later, Miles opened his brother's door to see Emily looking anxiously up at him.

'What's the matter, old thing?' he asked.

'Do you still want to sleep with me?' she asked timidly.

That same evening Vivien was alone, sketching good likenesses of Cad and Emily from memory. Next, she stood on a chair and took down one of her paintings from the wall. Having removed a faded envelope from the back of the frame, she carefully tucked it in the spine of a French novel which she placed in her case.

She paused for a moment at the door and gave a last quick look round the room, her eyes resting on the photograph on the mantelpiece.

'Sorry, Johnny,' she muttered softly, then spun on her heels and marched out of the room.

Faith always tried to make the send-off meal as British as possible. This time she was able to give the agents a feast of roast beef, roast potatoes and Yorkshire pudding.

'I never thought I'd see a joint like that again,' said Colin, pushing his plate away after two huge helpings. Faith couldn't help but notice that Emily only toyed with her food, pushing one particular piece of Yorkshire pudding round and round her plate. She was certainly the most anxious of the three.

What happens if the flight is cancelled?' asked Emily.

You all go home and wait to be summoned for another night,' Faith replied.

Emily stared at her soggy pudding and sighed. 'I couldn't bear that,' she said.

Vivien made short work of her meal and was enjoying a cigarette.

'I don't know,' she joked. 'If we get a send-off meal like this each time, I think I'll pray for fog!'

Everybody laughed nervously and then lapsed into silence, each one deep in his or her own personal thoughts. The long wait until take-off seemed an eternity as they sat round the cleared table, playing rummy.

After a game in which no one seemed to be concentrating very hard, the threesome cheered in unison as Faith came into the room and gave them the thumbs-up sign.

Down at Tangmere, Liz stood in the cold night air. She looked keenly up at the night sky, waiting for the arrival of the plane from France. Whilst she waited in the aerodrome, she wondered about the state of her marriage and why she felt this adolescent excitement at the prospect of seeing Kit again.

Laurence had hardly bothered to lift his nose out of *The Times* when she had said good-night. Did he believe her story, that she was on Outfit business? Or did he think that she would dress up in her FANY uniform to deceive him? Her sombre thoughts were interrupted by the unmistakable sound of a Lysander approaching. Immediately, her mind flashed back to France and those agonizing waits at improvised air-strips. The plane taxied safely to a standstill and out of the darkness a tall familiar figure climbed down from the plane.

Liz felt her heart leap with joy and she swallowed rapidly, trying to calm herself. She knew she couldn't run forward and embrace him as she wished to do; she would have to play the formal arrival committee part.

Kit looked amazed as she thrust her hand into his. She couldn't believe how tired and haggard he looked. Impatient of such formalities, he brushed her hand away and threw his arms around her.

'Oh God, I've missed you!' he murmured.

Tears came into her eyes. Eventually, she wriggled out of his embrace and led him back across the tarmac towards the car waiting to take him back to town. She felt quite sick; the person she most wanted in the whole world was beside her, yet she could not possibly show her true feelings.

CHAPTER 2

As the Lysander approached their destination, Vivien looked out with excitement at the dark outlines of the countryside below. She could see flares illuminating an improvised air-strip in the traditional L-shape, though none of the reception party was visible. Let's hope they are on our side, she thought, preparing to jump.

A cold rush of night air hit her as she followed Colin out of the plane. She pulled the cord on her flying-suit and heaved a sigh of relief when she felt the parachute open above her. Floating through the inky-black sky, she looked up. In the bright light of the full moon she saw Emily's parachute open and then – one by one – the three parachutes bearing the canisters which held supplies.

Vivien came to earth with a perfect textbook landing. Immediately, she unclipped the automatic release button and loosened the straps of her parachute. Then she removed her helmet and shook her hair free. Wriggling out of the 'striptease suit', she revealed the dowdy French outfit which she was wearing underneath.

She saw Emily some distance away on the edge of a tree-filled spinney. Typical Emily, Vivien smiled to herself. The young girl was already busy digging a hole in which to bury her parachute.

Vivien ran over to Emily, bundling up her parachute as she went.

'Wasn't so bad, was it?' she panted.

'Where's André?' asked Emily. There was no sign of the third member of their party.

'Dunno – but here comes our reception committee, by the look of it.'

Vivien watched as a group of five men dressed as agricultural labourers emerged from the cover of the woods and made their way towards them. A tall, wiry man led the party and stood waiting silently for Vivien to say something. She pulled herself together and spoke the passwords.

'Can you tell me where to find Auguste's vineyard?' she enunciated.

'Five kilometres to the west of the Mezin road,' replied the leader in a deadpan Scottish accent.

Vivien relaxed a little.

'Don't waste time doing that,' he snapped at Emily, who was still digging.

She looked up at him questioningly. 'But we were told to bury our . . .'

'Forget all that nonsense,' the Scotsman ordered. 'First thing they look for. Bring them with you; we'll dispose of them later.'

'I take it you're Gaspard,' Vivien said, more as a statement than a question.

'Ay,' replied the man gruffly. His real name was Gordon and he much preferred it; but Gaspard was the name he had been saddled with. He turned to the other men.

'Come on, don't stand around. Get everything loaded!'

The men rapidly gathered up the canisters with their parachutes attached; they contained ammunition, supplies and the team's luggage.

'Yours, I think,' said a shorter man with a moustache, handing Vivien a small, battered suitcase.

'I'm Josef,' he introduced himself. 'Resistance.'

'Solange.' Vivien held out her hand in greeting.

So this was the leader of the Resistance cell in Montaud. She much preferred the look of this man to the sour Scot.

'And this is Zoe,' she said, indicating Emily who had joined them.

'Welcome to France,' said Josef. 'We much appreciate . . .'

But before Josef could get any further, Gordon cut in. 'Never mind the chit-chat. Where's André?'

'He was the first out of the plane,' explained Vivien.

'One of them was a bit off-course,' put in another member of the Resistance.

'He may have landed in the river,' Josef suggested.

'Christ, that's all we need!' groaned Gordon.

An owl's hooting could be heard in the distance. 'Wait. That could be him!' said Emily.

'Well, it's no bloody owl, for sure,' Gordon growled.

'Careful,' cautioned Josef. 'It could be a trick. I'll go and look.'

'Me too,' volunteered Emily, to Vivien's surprise.

'Right. You two stay with me!' ordered Gordon, as Emily started to follow Josef into the trees.

Emily's heart beat so loudly that she was convinced that any German must be able to hear it for miles around as Josef led her through the woodland. As they crept through the long grass leading down to the river, the hooting became louder.

'André?' whispered Josef.

Emily stiffened.

'Over here!' Colin's voice came softly, from the river-bank.

'Thank God,' Josef sighed.

His torch picked out Colin, lying in the undergrowth and clutching his ankle. He looked extremely pale.

'Ankle?'

'Yes. Landed badly,' Colin croaked in pain. 'Tried to avoid the river.'

It was a slow and agonizing journey for Colin, back to the landing-strip. There Gordon and Josef loaded him into the lorry, while Emily helped Vivien and another Resistance member (who introduced himself as Louis) to finish loading the supplies into the back.

'For once, the French tittle-tattle's paid off,' said Gordon to Colin.

'How do you mean?'

'We spread it around that there was to be a raid on the railway junction on the other side of town. With any luck, they'll be out there in force.'

'We needed one piece of luck tonight,' said Josef, looking at the injured Englishman.

The safe house for the night was a small farmhouse several miles outside Montaud. The gnarled old farmer helped Josef and Gordon to hide the ammunition in his barn, while Emily tended to Colin in the kitchen.

Her background as a doctor's daughter came to the fore as she inspected the damage. Colin's ankle was swollen and rapidly turning a vivid plum colour; the pain was so excruciating that when she asked him to wriggle his toes the attempt reduced him almost to tears.

What a great start, thought Vivien grimly, as she busied herself tearing up rags to be used as bandages. We're not two minutes on French soil and this has to happen. The mood of fearful expectation which had reigned in the Lysander had already changed to one of depression and anxiety, and Emily's diagnosis was no comfort.

'I'm pretty sure it's a fracture,' she said, shaking her head. 'Best to treat it as one, anyway; that's what my father always says.'

She picked up the strips which Vivien had prepared and explained what she planned to do.

'I'll bandage it as best I can until we can get you to a doctor.'

'You'll be lucky,' snorted Gordon.

'I thought we had one working for us,' said Colin, remembering the background notes which they had all been given.

'Not any more; he was caught last week. And we daren't risk the hospitals – the Milice are watching them all the time.'

'If it's an ordinary fracture, it should heal quite easily,' said Emily, trying to reassure Colin. 'It's just a matter of resting it for a few weeks.'

Colin looked even more anxious. 'But I've got people to contact, all over the place,' he worried.

'Well, you'll have to leave that to *me*, won't you?' commanded Vivien. 'Just lie back and give the orders.'

Colin winced as Emily bandaged his foot.

'Want a fag?' asked Vivien, more sympathetically.

'Thanks. Jacket pocket.'

Vivien went to Colin's jacket which was hanging over the back of a chair and took a silver cigarette case out of the inside pocket.

'You'd better take one of Cad's pain-killing pills too,' said Emily.

'Unless you'd sooner take the suicide one,' said Gordon caustically.

Two women and a now-useless man clearly did not fill him with confidence. They all looked at him for a moment, then Vivien broke the tension with a laugh.

'I do like a dry sense of humour,' she said. flicking open the cigarette case and taking out two cigarettes. One she handed to Colin, the other she put in her mouth.

Gordon looked at her, appalled.

'Christ, you're not carrying that thing around, are you? They must be off their rockers back there. They talk about security, then dish out cigarette cases to every bloody agent. Why not just give us a visiting card saying "British Spy"?'

The following day, Vivien and Emily made their way from the farmhouse – for the first time seeing the sort of countryside that was to become their home. They trudged along a sandy, unmade road which ran through well-regimented vineyards. The vines followed the contours of the rolling hills and stretched way up into the distance. The track came to a T-junction with a signpost; it pointed in one direction to Montaud, which was two kilometres away, and in the other to Arbon, eight kilometres distant.

They stopped for a moment and put their cases down.

'The parting of the ways,' said Vivien, trying to make light of an important moment for both of them.

Emily gave Vivien a hug and looked up at her. Vivien saw that Emily was trembling.

'Be careful now,' said Vivien.

'And you.'

'No drunken orgies, mind!'

A shadow of a smile crossed Emily's face.

'And you'd better powder down those cheeks before

you get there,' added Vivien. 'Aren't you meant to have had TB?'

'See you tomorrow, as planned.'

'Yes, if I'm not completely crippled. Eight bloody kilometres!' Vivien exclaimed.

The two women hugged each other again, picked up their cases and set off in opposite directions.

Emily was oblivious to her surroundings as she set off alone towards Montaud in the warm sunshine. The early morning haze was lifting on another hot autumn day. The small mediaeval town of Montaud with its ochre brick walls and tiled roofs, stood high up on a hill dominating the surrounding countryside. Originally a 'bastide', a small fortified town, Montaud dated back to the time when the English ruled Aquitaine. Now it was a small sleepy market town.

To Emily, the two short kilometres felt like the longest walk that she had ever taken. On the way she went through her cover story over and over again in her head. She tried to think in French, but all she could think of was the most mundane English nursery rhymes. So she surprised herself when she spontaneously greeted a couple of Milice men who passed her on the outskirts of Montaud. They returned her 'Bonjour' and went on their way.

Her first little hurdle over, Emily gave an inward sigh of relief and set about looking for the Ferriers' shop which was situated in a narrow old-fashioned street. She looked through the shop window before entering and saw two women talking. There was nothing for it but to enter, so she opened the shop door and a little bell rang.

Marie looked up from her conversation with Annette and nodded at the newcomer, knowing immediately that this was their new lodger. She could have done without

Annette being there to observe everything. However, Emily smiled back and busied herself looking at the depleted stocks of kitchen ware.

Marie saw Annette glance at Emily with interest – here was a person she did not recognize. Annette had been trying to sell Marie all the clothes-pegs that she made to supplement her widow's pension, but Marie had had to explain to her that she could only take a few because people no longer had money to spend on anything other than the barest essentials. Annette's pleading had no effect, even though Marie felt sorry for the woman; she knew that the two dozen pegs she had taken out of pity would take a long time to sell.

Marie handed Annette money for the pegs and thought for a moment that she was going to say something; but Annette just put the money in her threadbare purse and made her farewells, giving Emily a second curious look before walking out of the shop.

Emily crossed to the shop counter and gulped.

'Madame Ferrier?' she asked tentatively.

Marie nodded, waiting for the password.

'I . . . I'm afraid I've forgotten what I'm supposed to say,' stammered Emily, blushing a deep crimson.

Marie smiled. 'It's about your cousin Leonie, I think.'

'Of course,' she said apologetically. 'I'm so sorry . . . I'm Zoe.'

'Wait there,' ordered Marie. 'If anyone comes in, you're buying something.'

Emily started to inspect the bottom of a saucepan as if it were a major masterpiece. She couldn't believe the gaffe she had just made. What on earth must Marie think?

Marie reappeared almost immediately with an old man, who wheeled his chair into the shop. Emily saw him look her up and down, and then smile.

'I am "Uncle Leon" from now on,' he said gruffly, shaking her firmly by the hand.

Marie seized Emily's small suitcase and led her upstairs to the tiny garret which was to be her new home. There were still a few signs of Luc's previous occupancy and a large picture of a school football team took pride of place. Emily looked round the room, taking in the bed, the small cupboard, and a chest of drawers on which stood a jug and basin. A crucifix hung over the bed. It was a simple room, but Marie had tried to make it welcoming. A small vase of wild flowers sat on the chest of drawers.

'It's a nice room,' said Emily sincerely.

When Marie explained that it had belonged to her son, Emily was most anxious that she had not dispossessed him of his room.

'No, no,' Marie assured her. 'He's not here any more. He went off last week to join the Maquis.'

Marie stood silent for a moment as she remembered the evening of his departure. He had joked about missing Emily, as he fancied English girls. He had never met an English girl in his life. Marie felt quite sick with worry about him.

'I haven't heard from him since he went,' she confided to Emily. 'I suppose I'll get a message eventually.'

Marie's mind returned to practicalities. 'There's running water in the kitchen. Lavatory's out there in the yard. I'm afraid it's not what you're used to.'

Emily warmed to this generous motherly figure. She wanted her to know how much she appreciated what she was doing, but Marie brushed her thanks on one side.

'It's we who should be thanking you. It's all we live for now, the Liberation.'

'I hope it won't be too far off.'

'Well, I'll leave you to unpack.'

'Oh, I'll need to go out later.'

Marie nodded. She knew that Emily would have to let London know that they had all arrived.

'Already?'

'They'll worry until we've made contact,' Emily explained. 'Josef said you had a bicycle I could use.'

'Yes. Where is it you've got to go?' asked Marie.

Emily hesitated for a moment; before she could say anything, Marie interrupted. 'You're right. Don't tell anyone anything. Come down when you're ready; I've made you some soup.'

Emily smiled at Marie and thanked her again. The Frenchwoman simply patted Emily comfortingly on the shoulder.

'Zoe, while you're here, just look on us as family.'

Marie then left the room. Emily blew her nose and started to unpack her case, hanging up her few clothes in the wardrobe. She looked round for a hiding place for her gun and – remembering Gordon's words – her silver compact.

As she came downstairs, Emily could hear Marie and 'Uncle Leon' talking in the kitchen.

'She's little more than a child,' he was saying.

Marie sounded only slightly more optimistic. 'She's older than Luc. Anyway, she wouldn't be allowed here if she wasn't twenty-one.'

Emily made a point of making a lot of noise as she came down the last few stairs, and then the three of them sat down round the kitchen table for a bowl of steaming vegetable soup and crusty bread. Emily hadn't realized how hungry she was. The walk in the country air had sharpened her appetite and she did not refuse Marie's offer of a second helping. She could feel Leon trying to sum her up and thought she would grow to like him despite his gruff approach. She already knew that she liked Marie.

Marie pumped up the tyres on the bicycle before handing it over to Emily. The two women walked up the passageway at the side of the shop.

'Make sure you're back by curfew,' Marie insisted in a whisper. 'The Milice are very strict on that.'

Emily got on the machine and cycled off, waving.

'I see you have a visitor, my dear.'

Annette's voice made Marie start; she had not noticed Annette creeping up behind her.

'My sister's girl, Zoe,' explained Marie hurriedly. 'She's staying with us for a while.'

'That's nice,' said Annette.

'She's not been well; her parents thought the change of air would do her good.'

Her passage back into the shop was blocked by Annette, who was eager to hear more.

'Would that be your cousin in Rochefort?'

'No. My second cousin, Robert. I told you about him,' Marie said stiffly. 'Remember? They were out in Martinique. And now I really must get on.'

Vivien took much longer than Emily to get to her safe house. What had started off as a pleasant country walk soon became painful, as her left shoe began to give her a blister. She had just taken off her shoe, sat down on the grassy verge and rubbed her foot for the umpteenth time when she heard the sound of a car approaching. Her heart seemed to turn a somersault as she saw it was a German patrol car, with an officer sitting in the back. Hesitating for only a split second, she jammed the shoe back on to her foot and stepped out into the road to hail the car.

'Thank heavens!' she exclaimed to the driver, when he leaned out of the car window. 'I thought no one would ever come!'

She smiled one of her most beguiling smiles. Instantly, one of the car doors was opened and Vivien was on her way in comfort.

The château stood at the end of a long drive with vineyards on either side. It was an imposing building, standing on a slight incline and dominating the surrounding countryside. A double flight of steps led up to the front door, which could have done with a lick of paint.

Hearing the sound of a car drawing up, a young woman holding a small baby on her hip walked round to the front of the house. Vivien recognized Juliette de Tramaut, the mistress of the château, with whom she had done much business during her wine-trading days. Her cover in France was to be that of Juliette's new nanny.

Juliette raised one eyebrow at Vivien's mode of transport and Vivien laughed. Then the two women embraced, and Vivien admired the baby.

Vivien waved goodbye to her German 'chauffeurs' and the two women went inside the château, to catch up with all their news.

'Kit doesn't look too good,' remarked Faith.

'No,' agreed Liz. trying to look busy with her work even though her emotions were in turmoil. Laurence had clearly disbelieved her explanation as to her mission the previous evening. It was ironic, she thought, that her reunion with Kit really had been in an official capacity.

'I'd like you to keep an eye on him,' Faith said.

‘Oh?’ Liz did her best to sound indifferent.

‘He’ll need a friend,’ Faith commented, studying Liz’s expression – or lack of it. ‘Someone who knows what it’s like.’

‘Actually, we’ve arranged to have dinner this evening,’ said Liz.

‘Good. Encourage him to talk about it all . . . and about his family. Trouble with someone like Kit, he keeps things bottled up. The psychiatrists were against sending him to France in the first place, you know.’

Liz looked up . This was the first she had heard of it. ‘Because of what happened to his family?’

Liz had known, of course, about Kit’s wife and children. On a visit to an aunt’s house in London, they had all been killed by a direct hit during a daylight air raid.

‘Yes. They felt he needed more time to grieve. But as Cad said, bereavement provides one of the strongest incentives.’

Liz nodded, remembering how much the death of her dashing elder brother Jack had spurred her on. A pilot who had failed to return from a mission over Germany, posted ‘missing’. The official line was that he had been blown up in his plane. The absence of a body to bury and lay to rest still haunted both Liz and her mother Evelyn.

Cad, too, was disturbed by Kit’s appearance. Dressed in his Army officer’s uniform, washed and shaved, Kit still looked dreadful. His hands shook as Cad offered him a cigarette.

Sitting back in his chair, Cad looked at Kit shrewdly. ‘We should have brought you back sooner,’ he commented.

'I wanted to stay,' asserted Kit.

Cad pulled luxuriously on his cigarette and leaned forward. 'Every time I had someone lined up to replace you, there was an emergency.'

Kit wanted to know about the overall situation.

'We're making an impression on the enemy now,' said Cad. 'But of course that leads to greater reprisals – as you know only too well. The loss of Maurice Granier's cell must have been a great blow.'

'It was mainly due to Maurice that I was able to keep things together.'

'Mm, we've a lot to thank those Commies for,' agreed Cad. 'Even if they're fighting for the Russians, rather than us.'

'It's not quite as simple as that, Cad.'

'It will be, once the war's over.'

Cad went on to tell Kit the good news about the Outfit's increased responsibility.

'We're to coordinate all our activities with High Command strategy,' said Cad, 'and the PM wants us to treble our effective circuits before the end of the year.'

Despite Cad's obvious pride, Kit merely shuffled his feet and looked disgruntled.

'A fine time to be called back!' he complained.

'We'll be needing you here, Kit. Your experience will be invaluable to us on the training side.'

'I'm not missing out on the invasion.'

'Let's see how it goes.'

'How what goes?' asked Kit testily.

'I don't have to tell you how grateful we are to you for all you've done, but now you need a good break.'

Kit glared at Cad and stubbed out his cigarette.

'You *must* have a break,' Cad continued. 'Take a month's leave. We'll talk about the future after that.'

The atmosphere at dinner was tense. Both Liz and Kit were trying to size each other up, unsure of where they stood. Even talk about mutual comrades in France brought about a momentary flash of antagonism. Kit felt that the Outfit's dislike and distrust of the Communists was an overreaction. He told Liz how Maurice had been captured by the Germans.

'He and some of the others were receiving an ammunition drop. The local Gaullists heard about it and turned up too. They started fighting over the stuff like a lot of kids; didn't hear the German's arrive. Most of them were captured . . . including Maurice.'

Liz looked at Kit, appalled. 'Did they shoot him?'

'They didn't need to. Not by the time the Gestapo had finished with him.'

They both sat in silence for a few moments, mourning their old friend. Then Kit looked up from his food and gazed round the room. He still couldn't believe he was back in the safety of England. The shared experience of France seemed like another world. Here he was sitting in dress uniform opposite a beautiful, stylish Englishwoman. They looked for all the world like any other couple dining intimately in an alcove in Albertina's.

Liz interrupted his reverie with a direct question about his plans. He shifted slightly in his seat and lit up another cigarette.

'I'll be moving into my club for the time being, then I'll probably visit the family estate. My brother will expect it.'

'What about your own house?' Liz asked tentatively.

'I suppose I'll have to go down there sooner or later.'

Liz leaned forward. 'Have you been back since Eleanor and the children were killed?'

Kit flinched. 'You know, you're the only person who . . .'

'What?'

'Spells it out. Eleanor; the children; what happened. Even Cad couldn't bring himself to talk about it.'

Liz pressed on. '*Have* you been down there?'

'No. I was away when it happened. They gave me compassionate leave to attend the funeral – if you can have a funeral without bodies. Then I went straight back to the regiment. Soon after, I joined the Outfit.'

'So the house has been shut up, has it?'

'Yes, the family solicitor arranged it all – and the disposal of their belongings.'

'You got rid of their things?' Liz was shocked.

'Yes!'

'I think you should go down there, Kit. Would it help if I came too?'

As he leaned across the table and grasped her hand she felt all the pent-up pain in him. straining to get out. Her pleasure at being with him was tempered by the knowledge of his extreme sadness. Somehow, she was convinced, she would help him come to terms with his loss and rebuild his life.

She still did not know if their affair was a thing of the past, a passion shared in the face of danger. Could it survive under calmer conditions? And *should* it? She thought again about Laurence, who had been surly and difficult for months, and knew that she was determined to find out.

It took Emily longer than she had expected to reach the

house where she would find her radio; she got lost on a on a couple of occasions and had to ask directions. Each time there was no hint that she wasn't passing as a native French speaker, and she allowed herself an inward sigh of relief. Her confidence began to grow as she cycled along and started to whistle one of her favourite pieces of Bach. This was a far cry from playing the organ in the school chapel, she thought wryly.

She had almost forgotten the danger that she was living in as a 'pianist' by the time she approached her destination – a small cottage surrounded by farm buildings. She parked her bicycle up against a large hen-house and walked up to the front door.

Emily almost fainted with shock as the door opened to reveal a uniformed gendarme. Certain that this must be the end, she managed to pull herself together and gave her password. To her great relief, the gendarme responded with the right phrase and showed her where the radio was hidden.

'In the hen-coop?' said Emily. 'How clever!'

There was the sound of a car approaching and the gendarme pushed her hastily inside the coop.

'German soldiers!' he hissed.

Quieter than a mouse, Emily crouched and listened as the gendarme exchanged pleasantries with the German soldiers. A shadow fell across a gap in the hen-coop door and Emily's heart stopped. Fortunately, it was just the Frenchman positioning himself so that no one could see inside. After a few minutes, which seemed like hours to Emily, the patrol car pulled out of the farmyard and away.

When the car had disappeared, the Frenchman let Emily out and she got down to the business of transmitting to London.

With the problems of finding the farmhouse and then the unexpected arrival of the German troops, Emily was late for her rendezvous with Colin and Vivien. When she arrived, Vivien was already well-established and making jokes about the basic duties of a nanny.

'Fill them up at one end and empty them at the other,' was how she described her job.

Colin sat on his bed with his foot raised on a stool. Emily gave his ankle a quick examination, while she told the others of her surprise at seeing the gendarme. He frowned and declared that Josef should have warned her; some of the ordinary police were in the Resistance, but it was difficult to know who to trust.

Colin's foot was on the mend, but Emily told him it would be some time before he could walk on it. He nodded resignedly.

It was well after blackout by the time Cad returned to Baker Street from his meetings at Whitehall. He found Faith still in her office, ploughing through a mountain of paperwork, with a half-drunk cup of cold tea at her side. He flung his cap down on a chair and began to loosen his tie.

'Thought I'd look in on my way home. Any news?' he asked.

'There's been a message through from Area 3.' Faith passed him a piece of paper. 'All well there.'

'Good,' grunted Cad.

'Nothing yet from Zoe in Area 7,' reported Faith.

'It's early days. She may not come through till tomorrow.'

'How was your meeting?'

'I suppose I'll get used to dealing with Yanks.'

'Was it constructive?'

'We were talking broad strategy tonight. Gil and I are meeting them again on Thursday to discuss specific operations.'

'Was the PM there?'

'Part of the time. He's anxious that we cooperate closely with de Gaulle's lot.'

'Easier said than done,' snorted Faith, who shared Cad's views on the Gaullists.

There was a knock on the door and a messenger poked his head round and handed Faith an envelope which she passed over to Cad. She looked at him anxiously as he opened it and read the message; then he smiled at her.

'They're okay,' he said.

'Thank God!' exclaimed Faith.

'They've made contact with Gaspard. Then there's something about Cyrano – something or other – what on earth's that word meant to be?'

He handed the message over to Faith, for her to try deciphering the word. She studied it for a moment and then saw what it was.

'Could it be ankle?'

Leon and Marie fretted, waiting for Emily to return. Three places were set in the kitchen for supper and they sipped anxiously at their glasses of local red wine as the vegetable stew simmered on the stove.

'It's nearly curfew,' muttered Leon grimly, as Marie got up to stir the food and prevent it sticking.

'I *can* tell the time,' retorted Marie.

They were both on edge. Only a minute before curfew, Leon tore off a chunk of bread and started to gnaw it anxiously. Each tick of the clock on the wall sounded like a death knell.

Suddenly they heard the sound of a bicycle being wheeled down the side alley and Marie dropped her spoon with relief. The back door opened and in walked Emily.

'And what time do you call this?' enquired Leon paternally.

The next morning, Marie gave Emily an overall so that she could help her in the shop. Almost as soon as the shop was opened, Annette came in. Marie was relieved to see how well Emily kept her composure and talked knowledgeably about Martinique, where she was supposed to come from. Her father was a sugar plantation manager and she had been sent to her aunt's to recuperate from TB. She excused herself graciously and went out the back of the shop.

Annette looked after the disappearing figure and then at Marie.

'Not much of a family likeness,' she observed.

'Takes after her mother's side,' laughed Marie. 'Far better-looking than the Jouvets.'

Annette looked unconvinced.

It was sunny as Kit and Liz motored down to Maidenhead. Kit was driving, but his mind was not on the road and all of a sudden, the car started to drift towards the centre.

'Careful. Wrong side!' warned Liz sharply.

'Blast!' exclaimed Kit, steering the vehicle back to the correct side of the road.

'Would you rather I drove?' she asked anxiously.

Kit still looked wan and grey.

'I must get used to it. Wasn't concentrating,' he explained.

The car rounded a bend and the Thames came into view. The water sparkled as sunlight hit it and a pair of swans glided past.

'When was the last time you came down?' asked Liz.

'August '41,' said Kit. 'I was home on leave. It was David's seventh birthday and we spent the day on the river. Three weeks later, they were dead.'

His face looked grim. They drove the rest of the way in silence.

The house was shuttered up, with blinds drawn and curtains pulled across the windows. Outside, a child's swing hung forlornly from a tree. Kit drew up opposite the front door and turned off the iginition.

'Would you rather I waited outside?' asked Liz.

'No,' said Kit, suddenly sounding as vulnerable as a small boy.

They got out of the car and stood together outside the front door, looking up at the house. Then Kit took out a large bunch of keys from his trouser pocket, dropping them as he tried to find the correct key.

Liz felt a little shiver go through her as they stepped inside the hall. It was eerie, laying other people's ghosts to rest, and she felt like an intruder.

The hall was bare except for a small chair and table covered by dust-sheets; there were marks on the walls where a mirror and pictures had once hung. Kit stood on the threshold for a moment, then strode to the drawing-room door and unlocked it. Inside it was murky and gloomy. Some furniture had been piled in the centre of the floor and covered with more dust-sheets. Liz walked across the room, pulled the curtains open and moved back the shutters.

Sunlight flooded into what once had been an elegant drawing-room. Kit looked under a dust-sheet at the assembled furniture, then replaced it. Slowly he led Liz around the house. He showed her every room, first on the ground floor and then upstairs. The empty nursery and bedrooms brought a lump to Liz's throat and she felt overwhelmed by Kit's sadness. A large, happy family house was now a cold, empty museum.

Kit paused at the top of the magnificent carpetless staircase as they finished their tour.

'Ordeal over,' he said softly. He turned to Liz. 'I'm glad you made me come.'

'How do you feel?' she asked, as they descended to the front hall.

'I don't feel anything. This has nothing to do with *them*,' he said, indicating the house with his hand. 'Let's go and get some lunch. There's a place along the river I—'

He broke off suddenly and Liz followed his gaze. Behind the front door, where they hadn't seen them when they first arrived, stood a pair of tiny black Wellington boots.

Kit turned away abruptly and went into the drawing-room. He stood holding on to the back of the sofa, his knuckles white as he tried to control his emotions. Liz walked slowly up to him and tentatively put her hand on his arm.

'Leave me alone,' he snapped. 'I'll be all right!'

He pulled away from her violently.

'No, Kit!' Liz cried out. 'You don't have to hide it from *me*. For God's sake, let it *go*!'

Gradually, Kit relaxed his grip on the back of the sofa and started to sob. His whole body shook with emotion as he turned to Liz and let her put her arms round him. She held him close and he leaned heavily on her as tears poured down his face.

After a time, his body no longer shook. She stroked his hair. Finally, he stood up straight and blew his nose.

'Oh God, Liz, I need you,' he exclaimed.

Then, almost as suddenly as the tears had stopped, he pulled Liz towards him and took her in his arms. They started to kiss, hungrily exploring each other. He fumbled with her blouse.

'Are you sure?' Liz pushed his hand away and looked at him questioningly.

'Yes, Liz. Yes,' Kit said urgently, pushing her backwards on to the dust-sheeted sofa.

Three weeks went by before Colin was on his feet, and even then he needed a walking-stick. His first rendezvous with Vivien away from his safe house was in Arbon, an attractive little market town which nestled in the rolling foothills leading up to the Pyrenees.

He found her waiting for him. Dressed in nanny's clothes, she sat rocking the pram gently backwards and forwards. She heard him coming before she saw him; the tapping of his stick echoed round the market square.

'So you've dropped your Elizabeth Barrett Browning act,' quipped Vivien, as Colin sat down on the other end of the bench.

'Now it's Long John Silver,' he replied bitterly.

'How do you account for the limp?' Vivien asked.

'I was injured in an air raid. Now I'm an insurance agent. I got my new papers yesterday; I hope to God they're OK.'

Vivien got down to business. 'Anything for Zoe?'

'Yes. And messages for Gaspard and Josef. They want us to get cracking on the sabotage training.'

He pointed to something in the newspaper he was

carrying and laughed loudly for the benefit of anyone who might be watching.

Vivien took the paper and also laughed. Then she carefully put it in the pram under the baby's blanket.

'You're the best-read baby in Arbon,' she cooed.

'He's smashing,' said Colin, peering into the pram.

Vivien looked at him sternly. '*He's* a little girl.' She gazed fondly at the baby for a moment, and then stiffened.

'Oh, oh,' she groaned as two Milice officers – one male, one female – came round the far end of the market square and walked towards them. Colin opened up his briefcase and hurriedly began to examine the insurance papers which were part of his cover. He turned to Vivien as soon as they were out of earshot.

'What's someone like that doing in the Milice?' he asked.

'Like what?' Vivien didn't know what he was talking about.

'Well – I mean – an attractive young girl.'

Were all her team totally naïve? wondered Vivien as she explained to Colin that collaboration was not peculiar to hatchet-faced males. He shut his briefcase and said that he would leave first, if Vivien would watch out to make sure that he wasn't being followed.

Colin had left the square and was walking slowly along towards the outskirts of the town when a voice made him start.

'Stop!' ordered a female voice.

Colin froze and turned to see the female Milice officer who had been in the square.

'Who? Me?' he asked.

'May I look at your papers, please?' the Milicienne asked in a businesslike tone.

Colin handed her his documents.

'I see you're exempted from forced labour,' she observed as she scanned the paperwork.

'Yes,' explained Colin, 'on health grounds. My leg – got smashed up in an air raid.'

'And now you work for an insurance company?' The policewoman read from his papers.

'There's enough bomb damage to keep us busy for years,' said Colin, hoping that he sounded convincing.

'How long will you be staying in this area?'

'I'm not sure. I've got a lot of people to see.'

'Don't forget to have these renewed if you stay longer than three months,' the woman said as she handed back his papers.

'Thank you,' said Colin, smiling at her.

He couldn't believe how young she looked; she was even younger than Zoe.

'Is it painful, your ankle?' she asked.

'Can't complain. At least I'm alive.'

'Yes. That's all that matters, isn't it?' The Milicienne spoke with startling ferocity.

After a couple of weeks, Colin was walking with only a slight limp. Nevertheless, he decided to keep using the walking-stick as part of his cover.

He and Gordon liaised with the Resistance and organized training sessions all over the Area. Colin sensed that the Scot was not that impressed with the team that had been sent out to join him.

Emily, in particular, seemed to be permanently ill. She felt terrible and presumed that it was the bug which had been going the rounds of the circuit. One by one, each of the team had gone down with a stomach complaint.

Transmitting and receiving became more and more arduous. She felt tired and sick as she crouched up in a barn loft listening to the transmission from England. She lay back for a moment's rest in the straw after she had packed away the aerial and put the radio back into its case.

However, her weariness lifted as she decoded the message she had received, and she felt full of excitement. The message gave some point to their all being there. According to London, situated right in the middle of Area 7 was a German transmitting station which could signal to submerged U-boats. It had been giving the submarines information about the Allied Fleet in the Atlantic, which had resulted in heavy losses. Cad's orders from the PM were for the circuit to blow up the installation, which would mean that the enemy submarines would have to surface to receive transmissions and thus would be easier targets for attack by the Navy.

Emily's excitement was shared by both Colin and Vivien as they pored over a map of the area in Colin's safe house. Vivien's talents as an artist were now to be put to use; on her 'day off', she would find out the lie of the land and produce sketches and diagrams. Colin asked Josef to find a contact inside the transmitting station.

The number of transmissions was raised to one every other day and Emily found this an increasing strain. One morning she wandered through Leon's work-room from the back-yard where she had been sick in the lavatory.

Leon greeted her gruffly without looking up from the battered typewriter which he was mending.

'You all right?' he asked.

Emily wiped her mouth with her hand and nodded.

'Yes, fine. It's just a slight stomach upset.'

'You British! A wonder your lips don't crack.'

'Do you want any help?' asked Emily, trying to change the subject.

'You couldn't do this sort of work,' snorted Leon.

'I bet I could. I'm always having to take my radio set to pieces.'

He thought for a moment and then indicated a dilapidated wireless at the end of his work-bench.

'See if you can get that going.'

Emily pulled up a stool and sat herself down next to Leon. She reached out for a screwdriver and started to examine the machine expertly as Leon watched her out of the corner of his eye.

The silence was eventually broken by Leon asking the question he had wanted to put to Emily for weeks. She was so young and vulnerable-looking that he wanted to father her; so doggedly determined that he couldn't help but admire her.

'What made you come out here?' he asked after Emily had finished mending the wireless and was sitting back admiring her handiwork.

She looked at Leon carefully and thought for a while before she replied.

'I suppose, for the same reason that you fought in the last war.'

Leon looked at the slip of a girl and said sadly, 'Well, I hope you don't end up like *me*.'

The news that Luc had reached the Maquis safe and sound sent Marie scuttling upstairs to share her joy with Emily, who felt the pleasure almost as much as if she had known the boy herself. She hugged Marie, delighted at the kind woman's relief.

'I wish you could have met him,' said Marie.

'Perhaps I will one day,' replied Emily.

'He's a fine lad; just like his father at that age.'

'Your husband . . . when was he . . .'

'Killed?' Marie finished off Emily's question. 'Right at the start. Yes, all the girls went for Luc.'

Emily smiled at the proud mother speaking.

'What about you?' Marie asked. 'Have you got a boy-friend back home?'

'Yes. We're not engaged or anything. I suppose we might eventually if . . . We can't make any plans at the present.'

'No,' acknowledged Marie. 'You've been sick again?'

'Wretched bug,' said Emily.

Marie looked at her young charge with concern. 'Do you *have* to go out?'

Emily nodded. 'Yes, I'm meeting someone.'

Hurrying through the streets of Montaud, deep in her own private world, Emily did not notice Vivien on the other side of the road pushing the pram along, nor the Milice officer standing on the corner of the street. She stood for a moment on the kerb and then stepped out in front of an oncoming car, which had to brake hard and swerve sharply to avoid hitting her. The driver wound down his window and directed a long stream of Gallic abuse at Emily, who quickly regained her composure and walked across to him to apologize for her stupidity.

Vivien had seen the incident; in fact, she had seen it coming. Emily had looked the wrong way before stepping off the pavement. Quick as a flash, before the car had even squealed to a halt, Vivien intercepted the Milice officer who had turned to see what the disturbance was about. As she asked for the whereabouts of a shop that sold baby clothes, she carefully positioned herself and the pram in front of him, thus blocking his view of the incident.

She engaged the man in idle prattle until she had seen Emily walk down the street and out of view.

A little later, the two women met as arranged, under a convenient archway.

'What on earth possessed you?' Vivien chastised Emily. 'It's the first thing we learnt on the course – don't look the wrong way when crossing the road.'

Emily looked shamefaced.

'I know,' she murmured.

'That weasel-faced officer was all set to collar you.'

'Please don't go on about it,' Emily pleaded.

'Well, I don't fancy prision visiting, that's all.'

'I wasn't thinking,' said Emily, shaking her head.

'That's not like you.' Vivien spoke gently to her young friend. 'You must take care, Zoe. We can't do without you.'

Emily took out her handkerchief and gave her nose a good hard blow. She then slipped a piece of paper inside it and leaned over the pram.

Saying, 'Baby's got a runny nose', she wiped the infant's nose with the hanky, then tucked it in under the blanket.

'I'll be off then,' she said to Vivien.

'You look lousy. Haven't you shaken off that bug yet?'

'I'm not sure.' Emily hesitated for a moment and then made up her mind.

'Can I ask you something?'

'Fire away.'

'You know what Liz Grainger told us about our periods – being a bit irregular?'

Vivien nodded. 'Tension and all that.'

'Well, I haven't had one since I came out here.'

'That's it then,' said Vivien in a matter-of-fact voice.

'Yes. Unless . . . you don't think it could be something else?'

Vivien looked at her in disbelief. 'But you couldn't be. *Could* you?'

One look at Emily's face answered that question and Vivien's jaw dropped in surprise. So much for the sweet young religious innocent!

'Bloody heck,' said Vivien.

The leaves were beginning to turn into their glorious autumnal colours of red and gold as Liz and Kit drove down to the country in his car. Liz had managed to wangle a few days of leave from the Outfit, having told Faith that Laurence was up north lecturing and that she would visit her mother in Devon to see Vicky. She had given her husband the same excuse.

Kit hummed softly to himself as they sped through the countryside and Liz was pleased to see that he had put on some weight. He seemed much less on edge and more at ease with the world. He refused to tell Liz where he was taking her, wanting it to be a surprise.

'Somewhere you've been before?' asked Liz.

'No, I wanted it to be *our* place, this time.'

Liz hoped that it wasn't somewhere she had been with Laurence . . . it wasn't.

The car drove through a small ford, sending wildfowl scattering. They rounded a corner – and there before them was a small, picture-book English village: a cluster of houses surrounding a village green, complete with duck-pond. Kit pulled up outside the largest of the buildings, a black and white half-timbered Tudor inn.

'Here we are,' he said, turning off the ignition.

'Oh, Kit!' Liz was touched.

He leaned across and kissed her. 'A far cry from France,' he said.

Liz's happiness was complete during those few stolen days in the country. They tramped for miles, each day setting out in a different direction. At night they ate hearty country fare in the pub, downed pints of beer and retired early to their four-poster bed.

They argued good-naturedly about everything. How unlike her relationship with Laurence, where they were both too polite ever to argue. Liz was slightly worried that Kit had become a Communist sympathizer whilst in France. They stopped a moment to look at the view, and Kit tried to explain his political perspective.

'Things will have to change after the war,' he told her. 'People won't be content with empty promises like last time: "A land fit for heroes" and all that.'

He noticed Liz scanning the horizon, her eyes resting on a long flat field. They suddenly realized both were thinking the same thought.

Liz laughed. 'Well, it would, wouldn't it? An excellent landing site!'

Laughing too, Kit seized Liz round the waist and spun her round and round, until she cried for mercy and they sank together, very slowly, to the ground.

Later the two of them lay on the grass, smoking and gazing at the overhead canopy of trees.

'I thought it might be . . . just France. You know, the danger and all that? But it wasn't,' said Liz, smiling.

Kit looked across at her.

'No,' he said, 'it certainly wasn't.'

All too soon, their rural idyll came to an end. Liz had to

appear at her mother's and also needed time on her own, without Laurence or Kit, so that she could sort out her thoughts. And most of all, she wanted to see Vicky again. Trudging the short walk from the station, she felt her heart lift as she saw her daughter playing by the front gate.

Liz dropped her case on the ground and rushed forward to greet Vicky. She swung her up in the air and hugged her close.

'I'm second tallest in my class,' boasted Vicky, who had grown considerably since Liz had last seen her.

'I've had to take all her hems down,' came the familiar voice of Liz's mother.

Liz embraced Evelyn. Then the two women each took one of Vicky's hands and they set off across the grounds towards the cottage where Evelyn was living. The main house, Northover Grange, had been requisitioned for the duration and now housed Canadian officers.

Later Liz and Evelyn sat drinking tea outside the cottage as they watched Vicky play. Evelyn was filling Liz in on all the local gossip, but soon became aware that her daughter was not listening.

'It's him, I suppose,' she said suddenly. 'That man you used to work with.'

Liz looked at her mother. She could never lie to her.

'Yes.'

'I thought you had it all under control?'

'So did I. Until he came back.' Liz tried to explain.

'Is that where you've been for the last two days?' asked Evelyn.

'How did you. . . ?'

'Laurence phoned for you yesterday. I pretended you'd gone for a walk.'

Liz sighed. 'I'm sorry. I didn't mean to involve you in the lies.'

‘Do you know what you’re risking?’

‘With him I feel alive. I need him, Mother.’

Evelyn looked hard at her daughter. ‘And Vicky needs you. You and Laurence. *Together.*’

‘I don’t love Laurence. I realize now that I never did.’

‘Being married never stopped anyone falling in love,’ said Evelyn sharply. ‘You get over it.’

Liz looked closly at her mother. ‘Did you ever have to make a choice?’

‘There isn’t any choice. Not once you have children.’

The two women slumped back into silence. Both of them watched Vicky playing without a care in the world.

Back in London, Liz found life increasingly unbearable. She was in a terrible state when Kit saw her next and deliberately chose to meet him by the Serpentine – somewhere not too intimate for what she had to do. She felt pulled in all directions and of no use to anybody.

When she told Kit that she wanted to call it a day, he stopped in his tracks.

‘Has Laurence found out?’ he asked.

‘He hasn’t said anything.’

‘Then for God’s sake, why? We can go on meeting, grab the odd weekend.’

Liz felt haggard, desperate.

‘And then what?’

‘Why think of the future when half the world’s dying?’

‘Things can’t stand still.’

‘Then get a divorce. Marry me.’

‘And what about Vicky?’

‘You left her to go to France!’ he reminded her.

'That wasn't just for *myself*,' said Liz miserably.

A passer-by looked curiously at the couple as their voices rose.

'How the hell can we talk here? Let's go somewhere else,' said Kit.

Liz resisted. 'No. It would only make things more difficult.' She gulped hard. 'I can't go on seeing you.'

Kit looked at her in astonishment.

'Do you think I'm letting you go just like that? Christ! Hasn't it meant anything to you?'

'Please,' she begged. 'Help me!'

Kit looked at her, then turned away abruptly. She watched his retreating figure and very nearly called after him to stop . . . but she didn't.

Colin came out of the front door of his safe house, pausing for a brief chat with the neighbour's children who were playing on the pavement. As he limped off up the street, he failed to notice a parked car on the other side of the road.

He walked through the picturesque town of Arbon, up to his rendezvous point with Gordon. The two men stood on the ramparts which overlooked the surrounding countryside. Vineyards stretched away on all sides, for miles and miles.

Gordon reported success at getting a team together for a raid on the German radio transmitting station, but said they were short of ammunition. Colin reassured him that another parachute drop was imminent.

They were just about to go their separate ways when Gordon mentioned that he had just seen Vivien going into the Town Hall.

'Curious, don't you think?' he said.

'A bit,' agreed Colin. 'But nothing to worry about.'

He was puzzling over this information as he hobbled down the steps from the perimeter wall and set off back to his lodgings. The children were still playing on the doorstep. He ruffled the youngest one's hair as he opened the front door, then made his way upstairs.

As he opened the door to his room, he saw someone standing by his bed going through his papers. The intruder turned, gun in hand. Colin went for his gun and both fired simultaneously. Colin felt a bullet go past his ear, and saw that his training had paid off.

The intruder dropped her gun and sank to the floor. With a shock, Colin recognized the woman Milice officer he had seen in the Square during his meeting with Vivien. Then, she had looked young and attractive. Now, she looked white, terrified.

'No,' she gasped in English. 'Please . . .'

She made a horrible sound, the first time Colin had ever heard a death rattle. Filled with dismay, he cradled her in his arms as the life flowed out of her.

CHAPTER 3

Vivien checked that no one was following her, then hurried through the town to Colin's safe house. She couldn't wait to see the expression on his face when she told him Emily's news. Gordon wouldn't be too pleased either; she could already hear his Scottish voice expressing puritanical condemnation.

Pausing on the landing outside Colin's room, she was surprised to see his door open. All thoughts of Emily disappeared – something wasn't right. She stood to one side of the door, then tentatively pushed it open and waited. Nothing happened. With a feeling of relief, she walked into the room.

Her relief was short-lived. Colin was motionless in the middle of the floor. He had his back to the door and was holding a dead woman in his arms. Smeared with blood, he sat bolt upright as if in a trance. Vivien knelt down beside him and took hold of his shoulder.

'It's me, André,' she whispered. 'Are you hurt?'

Colin stared blankly at her. Vivien found herself gagging as she saw the amount of blood everywhere. Colin's clothes were soaked in it.

'Come *on*!' she said urgently.

She tried to pull Colin away from the body, but he only

held on tighter and started to rock backwards and forwards as if the dead body were a baby.

Vivien recoiled and looked down at him, wondering desperately what to do. Finally, he registered Vivien's presence and gazed up at her forlornly.

'I think she's pretty badly hurt,' he whimpered.

'I'll get help,' said Vivien and hurriedly left the room.

She rushed downstairs, only just remembering to make herself stop to check it was all clear before she set off to find Gordon.

Initially Gordon was annoyed by her appearance at his work-place; his cover was that of a mechanic and he worked at a small garage on the outskirts of town. His colleagues looked curiously at Vivien when she asked to see him, and commented lewdly as she drew him aside for a private conversation. However, when she told him what had happened, he grimly acknowledged that she had taken the right action. Hurriedly making an excuse to the others he wiped his hands on an oily rag and jumped into the cabin of his engineering truck. As they drove back to Colin's safe house, they hurriedly worked out a plan of action.

Though still in a state of shock, Colin seemed at least to have regained the use of his legs. When Gordon told him that they needed to take the Milicienne to hospital, he nodded numbly. Vivien stood guard outside while the two men carried the body downstairs and lifted it into the back of the truck.

Gordon now had to clear the room of Colin's belongings. He suggested that Vivien stay in the truck with Colin, who was clearly in no condition to do any more.

'Got his papers?' asked Vivien, as Gordon climbed into the driver's seat beside them.

Gordon nodded and patted the pocket of his jacket.

Suddenly there was a familiar sound: a German patrol truck. Gordon swore and turned the ignition; and fortunately the engine started first time. They were only yards away as a German patrol truck pulled up outside the safe house. Vivien had a brief glimpse of a bunch of German soldiers with rifles who jumped out and started to kick down the front door.

Once Gordon had left the immediate vicinity, he slowed down, not wanting to attract undue attention. He drove out of Arbon and into a nearby wood.

'It's somewhere here,' he muttered.

Soon they rounded a corner and came to their destination. They were in an old disused quarry, full of water. Gordon parked the vehicle as close to the edge as he could.

For a moment, Vivien looked at the scene through artist's eyes. It was beautiful. The lake was a deep clear blue, and the sides of the quarry were a pearly, luminous white. The noise of Gordon heaving the dead woman out of the truck brought her back to reality. Although she had never liked Gordon, she had to admit the man was extremely capable.

'Can I help?' she asked, jumping out of the truck.

'Just keep a lookout,' Gordon told her.

He carried the body over his shoulders to the edge of the artificial lake, then collected some small boulders and tied them to it. Grunting with effort, Gordon pulled the dead woman into the water. As he did so, one of her shoes fell off and Vivien tried to help by jamming it back. By now, though, rigor mortis had set in and the shoe wouldn't go on. In exasperation, Vivien hurled the shoe into the middle of the lake. Gordon pulled the body further out from the edge, and let go. Slowly, the body slid under the water.

'Right,' said Gordon. 'Now to find a hiding-place for André.'

He took Vivien and Colin to the farmhouse where they had spent their first night in France. The farmer's wife greeted them warily, especially when she saw the state of Colin, but ushered them into the kitchen. There she produced a rough blanket to wrap round Colin as he sat by the kitchen fire – staring straight ahead, oblivious of anything going on around him. He brushed aside the acorn coffee which Vivien tried to persuade him to drink, and then finally spoke.

'She took so long to die,' he said.

The peasant woman eyed Colin suspiciously. She heard her husband returning from the fields, and went out into the farmyard to greet him. Vivien watched her go anxiously.

'It's all over now,' Vivien tried to comfort Colin.

'She was rather pretty,' he said.

'What?' asked Vivien in surprise.

'Like my mother. Years ago. She was pretty too.'

Vivien rounded on him. 'Come *on*, André! Think back to your training. Pull yourself together!'

The farmhouse door opened noisily and the old peasant burst into his kitchen. 'Did Josef send you?' He glared at them in anger.

Vivien recognized his face and greeted him warmly. She knew that she would have to handle him carefully; Colin looked as if he might be a great liability.

'Monsieur,' she said in her most engaging manner. 'You helped us before, I think.'

Her utterance was met with a stony silence but she pressed on.

'My friend needs a bed for a few nights. He isn't well.'

'Why? What's the matter with him?' the old man said sharply. 'Is he injured?'

'No.' Vivien shook her head.

The man relaxed slightly.

'Then what? What's he done? Hiding a few guns is one thing, but a man . . .'

Vivien decided to take a gamble and rounded on the farmer.

'Any true Frenchman would look after this man without all these questions! Josef made a mistake in you!'

The farmer looked down at his boots, and then up at Vivien. After a long silence, he spoke.

'Forgive me, it's been a hard day. My sons are . . . they were both . . .'

The unsaid word 'killed' echoed round the room.

'Don't worry,' he said. 'My wife will take good care of your friend.'

Vivien thanked him warmly and prepared to go. Looking back at the kitchen door, she saw that Colin had not moved from his position. His hands still held his bowl of untouched coffee.

The following day, Gordon unloaded his feelings about Colin to Emily. They had a rendezvous a short distance out of town, where Emily sat on the river-bank under a willow tree trying to summon up her courage to tell him about her probable pregnancy. The way he was striding up and down as he criticized Colin did not bode well.

'That type, they always crack,' he muttered. 'Of all the fool things to have done! Sitting there like a jelly on a plate . . . and with a dead Frog! Luckily for him, Solange came by and we got it sorted out.'

He came and sat down next to Emily.

'Yes, Gaspard.' Emily tried to steer the conversation round to her own problem. 'Did you wonder why she went there?'

'For messages. The girl's a courier.'

'And . . . she had some news, from me.'

Gordon looked at her uncomprehendingly.

'So I've got to tell you now,' she went on.

'Well? Make it good news. I could do with a break.'

Emily shook her head and gave him a wry smile.

'Sorry. The thing is . . . I seem to be pregnant.'

Gordon looked at her in disbelief. 'You're what? *Pregnant?*'

Emily just nodded her head.

'Bloody hell!' exclaimed Gordon, getting back on his feet. He started to walk up and down. 'That's all we need. No wireless operator. What a bloody shambles!'

'I'm sorry, but I'm not going back.'

'They'll have to send us a new man,' Gordon continued, without listening to Emily. But she got up and stood in front of him.

'I don't want to go home!' she insisted.

'And a pick-up for you. We'll get you home, don't worry.'

'Will you listen to me!' Emily shouted. 'I'm *not* going back. Not when I've just got settled, and I'm really needed.'

'And what do you think you're going to do, girl? You'll get as big as a bloody bus.'

Emily smiled at him and he looked at her seriously.

'It would be difficult finding a doctor for you. And then . . . a nursing mother in the field? It's just not on, lass.'

'I'm not leaving my post, whatever it takes,' she repeated stubbornly.

Gordon suddenly understood the implication of what

she was saying. 'Bloody hell, girl. I'll let the nobs work this one out!'

Emily's news cause pandemonium in Baker Street. On receiving the message, Cad strode into the office where Faith and Liz worked and threw the piece of paper on Faith's desk. She picked it up and read the message slowly. Liz was occupied in a long telephone conversation trying to get hold of some essential supplies. Faith put the message down and looked up at Cad.

'At least she wants to stay in the field.'

'Hopelessly naïve,' said Cad. 'After all the battles I had getting woman agents approved!'

'She's an inexperienced young girl, Cad.'

'Slightly too experienced, if you ask me.'

Liz put down the telephone receiver and looked questioningly at Faith and Cad.

'It's Emily Whitbread – Zoe. She thinks she may be six weeks pregnant.'

'God . . . What can we do?'

'What's the position on recruits?' asked Cad.

'There's nobody ready – or anywhere near ready.' Faith was angry. 'Her boyfriend might've taken better care of her!'

'She doesn't want him to know about it – and she wants to keep on working,' added Cad.

'There might be a way,' said Faith, half to herself.

'A back-street job? The old knitting-needles?' queried Cad. 'It's too big a security risk.'

Faith looked at him, shocked by his callousness.

'No, there's a pill now, but it's rather untried. It has to be taken before eight weeks.'

'And that would get rid of it?' Cad asked.

'Bring it on, yes.'

'But that would be . . .' Liz intervened. 'Would Emily do that? She's a Catholic, you know.'

'Damn!' Cad stubbed out his cigarette ferociously.

'She might,' said Faith, 'if she understood how important it is to us.'

'We've two drops tomorrow night: Areas 2 and 7,' said Liz.

'It might be possible,' commented Faith, looking at Cad.

'Make doubly sure that thing gets to her tomorrow,' ordered Cad. 'The situation in Area 7 is bad enough without complications like this!'

He left the office, slamming the door shut behind him, as Liz looked at Faith.

'Poor Zoe. What must she be going through?'

'I know. I just hope we can get hold of this pill today, for her sake.'

'I'll do it, Faith. Where's the medical file?'

'We'll certainly need a full moon tomorrow,' mused Faith, returning with difficulty to her paperwork.

'Don't worry. I'll get it. Then I have to tie up some loose ends for the agents flying out to Area 2.'

'You won't mind seeing off Gerard and Philippe?'

'Of course not.'

'You don't have to take on so much, you know.'

'But I want to.'

Faith looked at Liz with concern, sensing that Liz was going through an emotional crisis and was obviously trying to avoid confronting it by taking on increasing amounts of work.

Liz managed to track down the pill for Emily, but that

involved her in driving out of London to East Anglia. It was late at night by the time she arrived home, and Laurence was sitting up in bed reading legal reports when she tiptoed in. She had rather hoped that he would be fast asleep, so that she wouldn't have to undergo his frosty cross-examination of her every movement.

'I suppose it was too much to expect a telephone call,' Laurence sighed in a long-suffering manner, setting his documents on one side.

'You weren't here,' snapped Liz, all her good intentions towards him disappearing out of the window. She was drained and exhausted. 'And I did try, around seven.'

Laurence acknowledged the possibility that this was true, but continued to moan.

'Well,' he said, 'there wasn't anything to eat in the house.'

He picked up his papers and continued reading and Liz wondered for a moment whether to make an issue of it. Hanging up her coat in the wardrobe, she decided against prolonging the argument but crossed the room and sat on the edge of the bed.

'Sorry. You did have some dinner?'

Laurence kept on reading.

'Eventually,' he grunted.

There was a pause, and then he looked at Liz.

'Did you?' he asked belatedly.

Liz picked up her dressing-gown. 'I wasn't hungry.' She paused at the bedroom door on her way to the bathroom. 'I'll be out tomorrow, all night. Then I'll go straight on to HQ.'

There was no response from her husband.

'We're sending some new people out,' she added.

Laurence merely continued reading.

The message from London made it clear to Emily that she had no alternative. Much to her surprise, however, Vivien tried to persuade her to have the baby.

'Listen to me,' said Vivien. 'If you do this, you'll regret it for the rest of your life.'

'You can't know that,' Emily argued.

'I can. Oh yes, I can.'

Emily looked closely at her friend.

'It happened to me,' explained Vivien, 'when I was about your age. My dancing days. With a bun in the oven!' She gave a brittle laugh.

'What did you do?' asked Emily.

'A friend helped me; it was before I married Johnny. I hid away in the country, a very quiet little place.'

'You had the baby?'

'She was taken away from me and adopted. They didn't even show her to me.'

'You said you'd never had any children.'

'John always thought I was the one who couldn't. Well, it's too late now. It never occurred to me that I might not have another kid. Go home and have it. Do what *you* really want.'

'I can't.'

'Don't you love Miles?'

'I do miss him.'

'And what about your Church?'

'Don't, Solange!' Emily had tried to push this aspect to the back of her mind.

Vivien leaned back in her seat and groaned.

'God – women's lives!'

'I know how much you disapprove, but I've got to do it. I'm scared, Solange.'

Back at the château, Vivien dropped back into her role of nanny and soothed the infant in her charge. She thought sadly about Emily, and about her own child whom she had never seen. Suddenly she came to a decision, checked that she was the only person in the house and picked up the telephone in the hall. After a lengthy wait, she was eventually connected.

'May I speak to Father Giraud, please?' she asked.

The wait seemed interminable to Vivien, until she heard an elderly voice at the other end of the line.

'Father,' she said. 'I have to see you, it's very important . . . No, I can't talk on the telephone.'

Swiftly she arranged to visit the priest in his vestry the following afternoon.

That evening, she cycled over to make her contact with Colin. Dark had already fallen as she pedalled hurriedly towards the isolated farmhouse where he was still hiding. As she travelled along a country lane surrounded on both sides by oak woodland, the road grew narrower and the trees seemed to be closing in on her in the darkness.

Vivien rarely felt frightened; but her heart leapt as she heard a truck come up slowly behind her. For a time, it followed; she did not dare to look round. Then it put on a spurt and overtook her, only to stop some distance up the road. She continued cycling, her heart pounding away. Anything could happen to her in this deserted place.

As she drew alongside the truck, a familiar voice spoke her name. It was Gordon. She sighed with relief and got off her bike. He leaned out of the cab window and whispered to her.

'You're late – you should be there with Cyrano by now.'

'I know,' Vivien muttered.

'Throw the bike on,' ordered Gordon.

Vivien was only too delighted to follow his instructions and heaved her bike on to a pile of logs in the back of the truck. Then she hauled herself up into the cab and sat beside him. He started the engine and they drove off through the woods.

'Did you meet Zoe?' Gordon asked.

'I think she's making a big mistake,' replied Vivien.

'It's her choice,' said the gruff Scotsman.

'She's got *no* choice,' retorted Vivien angrily.

'She's a good lass; we need her just now.'

'Is that all you can think of? To you she's just a piece of machinery: not even a person any more!'

Gordon pulled up sharply and turned on Vivien.

'Don't talk baloney! And what is it to you anyway? You're very jumpy. What's the matter, Solange? Are you hiding something? Is it about the drop tonight?'

Gordon stared at Vivien, his face full of suspicion. Unable to respond, she sat angrily silent. Suddenly the silence was disturbed by the sound of an approaching aircraft; it was a Halifax bomber.

'Hell's bells!' exclaimed Gordon. 'It's here already – It's not due till eleven!'

When they reached the drop, they discovered that Colin had managed to assemble only a small group of helpers. Gordon was angry and turned on Colin, who seemed withdrawn and silent. Josef explained to Gordon that the numbers were depleted because it had been unsafe for many of the men to come.

'Jesus wept!' swore Gordon, looking at the number of containers which had been dropped. 'How do we get this lot to bed before dawn?'

He waited for a response from Colin. Vivien, Louis and a couple of others were already collecting the containers which had been dropped by parachute.

'Come on, man!' Gordon hissed at Colin, who merely continued to stand at the edge of the airfield, staring up at a nearby tree. A parachute was tangled up in the branches and it flapped in the breeze.

'Look at that, look at that,' Colin was murmuring.

Gordon spotted that the container beneath the tree was marked with a white cross. This meant that inside it, along with guns, was the pill for Emily. He loaded the container into the truck.

As if in a daze, Colin prepared to climb the tree to bring down the parachute and remove this evidence of the drop. He found a foothold on the trunk and grabbed a branch above his head. As he began to hoist himself up, however, he gave a cry of pain and fell to the ground.

Vivien hurried over to help as he rolled about on the ground gripping his ankle, which had given way.

'What is it? What's wrong?' she whispered.

Gordon joined them and stared down in horror at Colin who was crying helplessly, completely out of control.

'Loco,' said Gordon. 'Pure loco.' He turned to Vivien. 'You'll have to look after him,' he continued contemptuously. 'I'll get the men organized.'

Liz's send-off to Area 2 had to be delayed at the last minute when an urgent message came in, warning that the Germans knew it was imminent. She drove back to

London – partly dissatisfied, partly relieved that after all she would be able to have an early night.

Nevertheless she wondered whether she would get any sleep. All the adrenaline which invariably built up before a departure was still pumping through her. Yet she felt immensely tired as she climbed the stairs to her mansion flat.

Letting herself in, she tiptoed up the corridor towards the bedroom. There she opened the door and stood for a moment, letting the light from the hall illuminate the room, not wanting to disturb Laurence. He stirred in the bed and looked up from the pillow.

'Sorry,' whispered Liz. 'I'll just get some things.'

It was only when she noticed the strange expression on his face that she noticed he was not alone. Laurence sat up and Liz saw, lying next to him in her place, a blonde-haired woman. Liz turned on her heels and ran out of the flat.

Faith pulled on a dressing gown and went to open her front door. A wan and tearful Liz stood there clutching her handbag.

'I couldn't think of anywhere else to go.'

Faith ushered Liz inside and took her hat and coat. Then she hugged the forlorn woman and took her into her simple but elegant drawing room. Walking over to a small antique side-table, she picked up a cut-glass decanter and poured out two large drinks. Liz sat on the edge of the sofa, knocked back the first glass and held it out to Faith to refill.

'So what happened?' asked Faith, passing Liz a second drink.

'They were in our bed! Whoever she is – to bring her

home like that! How many times has he done that, brought some woman back while I wasn't there? I thought I knew Laurence.'

Liz rose from the sofa and walked across to the window, where she tweaked open the blackout curtain and looked outside. Dawn was beginning to break across London; the clouds were wisps of pink. She drew back the curtains and let daylight flood into the room, then stood nursing the glass in her hands.

'He was acting like the injured innocent, all this time. And all the time – with Kit – I felt so guilty. Poor *Laurence*!' she snorted. 'If I'd known, Kit and I would still be together. Damn Laurence! Now it's too late . . . it's just too late.'

As soon as all the guns and ammunition were hidden away, Gordon returned to the farmhouse.

'It's a miracle we got the stuff away,' he told Colin. 'That drop was a bloody shambles.'

Colin paused for a moment by the window and looked out at the farmyard coming to life.

'I know they'll come and get me,' he said mournfully. 'I know they will.'

'What?' Gordon sounded brusque. Colin seemed to be making no sense at all.

'You see, I don't sleep now at all. If I shut my eyes . . .'

Gordon tried to talk sensibly to Colin, but the man just rambled. All he could talk about was the death of the Milicienne, repeating the details over and over again. While Gordon felt sorry for him, something had to be done to keep the circuit together.

'I'm sorry, André, but this is no good. You're a security risk, London's got to be told.'

He walked across the room and came up behind Colin quietly. 'Because you're not getting better, are you?' he said in his ear.

Colin jumped and let out a little cry. 'I see her face. She won't let go.'

'Like I said, André, there's a job to be done here. So I'm taking over. Do you agree?'

Although not out on the drop, Emily had also had a sleepless night struggling with her conscience about the baby. She thought of the dilemma from all the angles: what did she want to do, what should she do, what would her father have suggested, what would a priest . . .? After several hours of worry, she got out of bed and – for the first time since she had been in France – knelt in front of the small wooden crucifix hanging on her bedroom wall.

In the morning she felt dreadful; but for once business was good, so she had to help Marie in the shop. When Vivien entered, Emily only just remembered not to greet her. Vivien produced a clock from her shopping basket and placed it on the shop counter in front of Emily.

'It's as dead as a doornail,' Vivien said.

'My uncle will have a look at it,' replied Emily, writing out a repair ticket.

'Can I have an estimate?' Vivien asked.

Emily realized that Vivien wanted to talk, and asked her to come through into the workshop. Leon looked up from his work as the two women entered, then returned to the radio he was mending. Emily put Vivien's clock down on a bench and started to open up the back with a screwdriver.

Vivien spoke quietly. 'It's in there. And one other thing – Gaspard's decided he's boss for now.'

Emily looked surprised. 'What's the matter with André?'

'He's in a bad way, after last night. Gaspard wants them to send a pick-up.'

'But he might get better?'

'Not if he stays here, I reckon.'

Emily thought for a moment and then sucked in her cheeks and blew out a gasp of air.

'Gaspard as leader!' she said in dismay.

Easing off the back of the clock, she gingerly took out the small package hidden inside, slipping it into the pocket of her overall without opening it.

Vivien touched Emily's wrist gently. 'Stop and think it over, Zoe; it's still not too late.'

When Vivien had gone, Emily took out the package from her pocket and opened it up to reveal a small pill-box. She glanced guiltily towards Leon and thrust it back. Also in the package was a brown envelope and Emily looked at the handwriting in surprise; it was Miles's rounded scrawl.

Leon asked her to pass him a soldering iron and as she handed it to him he noticed the letter in her hand.

'A letter from your family?' he asked kindly.

'No,' said Emily quickly. 'It's from my boyfriend.'

Suddenly she burst into tears and dashed out of the workshop and up to her bedroom.

Not surprisingly, Liz was unable to concentrate on her work at Baker Street. In the end, Faith told her not to wait around but to go home early and pack her things.

Although Laurence was there, Liz could not bring

herself to speak to him. He too seemed lost for words, and hung around by the bedroom door as she packed her suitcase. In her present state of mind, she was not particularly interested in what she took. She glanced at a ballgown which hadn't had an airing since war began, and wondered whether to take it with her.

'You had said you wouldn't be home,' Laurence explained, as if it had been Liz's fault.

'The flight was cancelled.'

Liz then put the question which she knew she shouldn't ask. 'How many other times. . . ?'

Laurence looked at her like an injured Labrador. 'We didn't have anywhere else to go.'

'And . . . how many other women?'

'Don't be ridiculous . . . or so insulting. Alice is not other women.'

Liz began to realize that she had been displaced in more ways than one.

'But in our bed?' She was astonished at his lack of sensitivity.

'What's so sacred about that?' retorted Laurence. 'You've been deceiving me for months. Did you think I hadn't noticed? Don't try to blame me for everything now!'

Another flood of pain overwhelmed Liz as she tried to account for herself.

'It wasn't months, Laurence. We had very little time together.'

The bitterness of his expression appalled her and she turned away to continue her packing. She looked down at the small balls of rolled-up stockings that lay on top of her clothes.

'Who is she?' she asked.

'She works at the War Office. Her husband was killed in '41.'

'All those trips away . . .?'

'Sometimes. Alice works as a driver and secretary.'

'That's cosy.' Liz couldn't refrain from the snide rejoinder.

'She has a young son, a seven-year-old. I've got to do the decent thing, Liz; I want to marry her.'

Liz stood still, gradually absorbing what Laurence was saying. Then she turned to look at him.

'I feel very badly about the position she's in,' continued Laurence, despite Liz's look of contempt. 'She's a respectable woman, and a fine mother. I'm sure you can see . . .'

Liz snapped the case shut, lifted it off the bed and carried it out to the hallway.

'Where will you stay?' he asked.

'That's nothing to do with you now.'

'Of course,' said Laurence. 'With him.'

'No!' Liz was furious. 'Because it's over. I sent him away, for Vicky's sake and for yours.'

'You don't expect me to believe that!' bellowed Laurence, as Liz marched into the drawing room.

She stalked over to the bookcase and searched for a particular book to take with her. 'Believe what you like,' she said over her shoulder. 'You used not to be so cynical.'

She found what she was looking for and put *The House at Pooh Corner* into her handbag, only half-hearing Laurence's accusations.

'I had to learn to distrust you, to live with all the lies. Do you realize what that job has done to you? I came back from Cairo to find a stranger. You ignored me. All I ever wanted was a wife to come home to.'

'A wife,' snorted Liz.

'I waited. I gave you every chance.'

He walked across the room and pulled her round by the shoulders so that he could look her straight in the face. 'He was someone you worked with, wasn't he?' he demanded.

Liz shook her head sadly. 'That isn't relevant now. I finished it . . . so that we could try again.'

But Laurence wouldn't let go. 'Were you together in France?'

'For a while, but . . .'

'What's his name?'

'For God's sake!' she muttered. 'You're not in court. Keep him out of this.'

Laurence's voice changed and became ice cool.

'That . . . may not be possible,' he said. 'You see, you wronged me first.'

'You can have your divorce, Laurence. I won't stand in your way. But I'll tell Vicky myself.'

He shook his head. 'She's been through too much already.'

'What do you mean? Boarding school?'

'Because of you going away, deserting her. You're not fit to be a mother – not now. You stopped putting her first, as well as me. She deserved better! Alice is a wonderful mother, devoted.'

This was more than Liz could bear. Infidelity she could cope with, but to have judgement passed on her like this was too much.

'Vicky needs a proper mother – not one with your kind of priorities. We shall have her,' Laurence was saying.

Liz felt the primitive instincts of a mother to protect her young rise up in her.

'Oh no, you won't!' she shouted.

'Then I'll drag the whole story through the courts.'

'But that would hurt Vicky!'

Laurence looked at her coldly. 'You know what to do then.'

She removed a small framed photo of Vicky from the mantelpiece and put it in her handbag, then stalked out of the drawing-room and picked up her suitcase. Struggling with her emotions, she tried to make a dignified exit. She had opened the front door and was about to slam it shut when she gave expression to her rage.

'I'll never give her up.' she screamed from the doorway. *'Never!'*

Before she could catch the bus to keep her appointment with the priest, Vivien had to meet Gordon. They sat outside a café in the market square. If she had not felt so tense, Vivien might have enjoyed the sunshine; as it was, she drank her coffee with increasing frustration. Gordon had spoilt all her plans for the day. As well as delivering a number of messages, he wanted her to go and check that Zoe was all right.

For his part, Gordon was surprised at Vivien's transparent irritation at being given orders by him. Beginning to have severe doubts about her attitude, he said goodbye curtly and got up from the table.

Vivien waited for him to disappear from view, left a few pieces of small change on the café table and set off for the bus station. She was sure that Zoe could look after herself for one afternoon.

The slow, bumpy bus journey was interminable. The vehicle seemed to stop at every village and hamlet, many of whose names Vivien recognized from her days in the wine trade. As the bus meandered off the main road, through the neatly regimented rows of vines and small holdings, Vivien wondered what the vintage would be like. This was superb wine country. It was such a shame that the Germans took all the best for themselves. Vivien cursed her luck when the bus was flagged down by some German soldiers just outside the town of Casterac, her destination.

She clutched her basket tightly as the soldiers walked down the bus, checking everyone's identity papers. The basket contained the English novel which she had smuggled into France. As she handed over her papers, she smiled sweetly and crossed her legs to show them to their best advantage. The soldier gave them only a brief glance before turning to an old peasant man sitting opposite her; his fingers were trembling as he took out his ID.

The other passengers turned away, too frightened to look, as the German soldier ordered the old man off the bus.

By the time that Vivien reached her destination, she was late for her appointment. She sat at the back of the Church by the main door, quietly watching a baptism take place.

Father Giraud said farewell to the proud parents at the main door and went back to tidy the font. After a few more minutes, he looked across at Vivien, as if to see whether he recognized her. Pausing first to genuflect in front of a side altar ablaze with candles, the priest came and sat on the chair next to her.

'I'm sorry you have had to wait,' apologized the old man.

Vivien took out the novel from her basket and opened it up. She removed the hidden documents and unfolded them, trying to smooth out the creases.

'You won't remember me,' she whispered as she

passed the priest the papers. 'It was nearly twenty years ago.'

'So much has happened in recent times,' the priest sighed, getting out his spectacles and beginning to read the faded documents.

'I was very young. I had a child. My daughter. You advised me to give her up for adoption.'

Father Giraud frowned, trying to recall Vivien.

'You surely know her well,' Vivien continued. 'You must have watched her growing up: the daughter of Henri and Marguerite Moreau. She'll be almost nineteen now.'

The priest nodded his head in recollection. 'I'm sorry to say they've moved away from here.'

Vivien groaned with disappointment.

'Three or four years ago,' continued the priest, 'when the war began. Of course I knew her well. Yvette Moreau.'

'Yvette?'

'If I remember aright, she was baptized Yvette Thérèse.' He nodded. 'A good Catholic girl, up until the war. And now? Who knows?'

Vivien looked at the priest intensely. 'Where did they go?' she demanded.

The old man thought for a while, then shook his head.

'I've *got* to know!' Vivien was almost crying with frustration.

The priest flapped his hands.

'Where is anyone these days? So many lost and scattered. I'm sorry.'

'I lost my husband; the Germans killed him. I was never able to have children after Yvette. She's all I've got,' pleaded Vivien.

'If I could help you, I would,' said the priest, patting her knee by way of consolation.

'I've thought of nothing but her. To know that she's safe . . . and that it worked out for her. Do you understand?'

'She has her own life: a mother and a father.'

'I only want to see her. *Somebody* must know where the family's gone,' pleaded Vivien.

She sat in an agony of expectation as the old man thought. Finally, he nodded and promised to make enquiries.

Back in Montaud, Emily had made her decision.

After lunch, she went upstairs to her room and took out the small pill-box from its hiding place. She sat for a short time on the edge of the bed and then, plucking up courage, took out the pill and swallowed it with a great gulp of water.

Back downstairs, she resumed helping in the shop. Marie had decided to do a spot of unseasonal spring cleaning, and Emily was standing on a chair to dust the top shelves when she felt the most appalling wrenching pains inside her. She tottered from the chair and sat down on it, clutching her stomach in agony.

Marie rushed out from behind the counter and knelt down beside Emily.

'I know what it is,' she said, putting her arms around the girl. 'You've been sick every morning. You're pregnant, aren't you?'

'I was,' said Emily, trying to hold back the tears.

'You're losing it?' asked Marie anxiously. 'Oh, why didn't you tell me?'

Emily got up from the chair and started to walk towards the back door, but she had barely moved two paces before she buckled at the knees. When Marie rushed over to support her, Emily looked up at the motherly woman in shame.

'I'm sorry. I don't want to be any trouble.'

Marie was appalled at the plight of the young girl, clutching her sides in agony.

'You've taken something, haven't you?' she questioned.

Emily could barely choke out the 'Yes'.

'What was it?' Marie asked.

Emily just shook her head. She had no idea what she had taken.

'Your people should be here. How could they leave you on your own?'

'It doesn't matter,' Emily sobbed. 'I've got to get it over quickly.'

'Lean on me,' said Marie soothingly. 'Come with me and don't be frightened. God will look after you.'

She helped Emily out through the workshop and into the backyard. Leon, who had heard everything, followed them in his wheelchair.

'My goodness!' said an all-too-familiar voice.

Leon spun round in his wheelchair and, to his horror, saw Annette coming down the side alleyway. He had the presence of mind to wheel himself between her and the outside lavatory, into which Marie had disappeared with Emily.

'Whatever's wrong with Zoe?' Annette continued.

Hearing Annette's voice, Marie left Emily slumped in the little shed and hurried across to make sure Leon was not being too rude to their neighbour.

'It's a touch of colic. Something has disagreed with her,' she explained, indicating to Leon that he should go off and mind the shop.

‘Can I do anything? Do you want me to fetch the doctor?’

‘It’s kind of you, Annette, but no thanks.’ Marie tried hard not to show her irritation.

‘But you never know, Annette pressed on, ‘it might be something she’s brought back from the tropics.’

‘Annette!’ snapped Marie. ‘You know we can’t afford the doctor. It’s just a stomach pain, that’s all. I’ll let you know how she is later.’

Marie turned her back on Annette and walked into the shop, where Leon was serving a customer. Once they were alone, Marie asked for some of the morphine which Leon took occasionally. He handed her his bottle and asked whether Emily would be all right.

‘I don’t know,’ replied Marie. ‘Those people are barbarians, leaving her alone at a time like this!’

Outside in the shed, Emily managed to swallow a mouthful of Leon’s medicine before the cramps bent her double again.

Liz was stunned by Laurence’s attitude. With his lawyer’s mind, he had hit unerringly on her most vulnerable point: her feelings of guilt that her career had left her little time for Vicky. There might be nothing left of her marriage, but Liz was determined that Laurence would not alienate Vicky from her.

It was an awkward time to leave the office. Cad had just heard from Area 7 about André’s breakdown and knew he would have to be got out. He prowled round the office like a balding bear with a sore head, snapping at Faith and Liz as if they were somehow personally responsible for the lack of fresh recruits to replace Colin. Liz felt a pang of guilt about leaving the office, but she had to get down to Vicky's school. She was determined that Laurence should not be the first to tell their daughter about the divorce.

Liz trudged the long walk from the station to Vicky's school. Pausing for breath by the tall railings, she caught sight of Vicky in the distance, playing happily with a group of little girls. Her face lit up at the sight of her daughter, and she quickened her step towards the entrance. As she did so, she saw a teacher come out of the school and call Vicky over. The little girl started walking towards her and then broke into a run; Liz watched with dismay as Laurence appeared at the teacher's side.

Vicky ran up to her father and flung her arms round him. He lifted her up and swung her round in the air and then hugged her close to him. She clutched his hand as they walked towards his car where a tall blonde woman stood waiting.

Liz caught her breath. So this was Alice.

Alice bent down to have a word with Vicky and was rewarded with a kiss on both cheeks. Liz winced at the knowledge that this was not their first meeting . . . worse still, Vicky obviously liked the woman.

As Liz leaned back against the school wall, all her resolution drained out of her and tears started to her eyes as she watched Laurence's car swing out of the gates. Vicky and Alice were chattering happily in the back and Laurence was joining in with their laughter as he drove along. The car roared past, the occupants oblivious of the desolate figure that they left behind.

Liz took several deep breaths and tried to pull herself together. Laurence's words of condemnation rang round her mind. Maybe there was some truth in what he had said, but if she couldn't be a mother she could certainly be of use elsewhere. She returned to London full of purpose, determined to speak to Cad before he left for the night.

Faith was furious with Cad when he told her that he had decided to accept Liz's offer.

'Liz has lost everything,' she expostulated. 'She has no reason to come back alive. What would the psychiatrist make of that?'

'A similar motivation worked well for Kit Vanston, and others too. Solange, for example.'

'Liz is different.'

Cad sometimes thought that Faith was far too fond of Liz.

'To you, perhaps. God knows, we need her out there. She's a damn good agent.'

Faith reiterated her point.

'She's deeply disturbed at the moment. You've given her no time to think. Tomorrow, indeed!'

Faith looked at the door which Cad slammed shut and thought for a few minutes. Picking up the telephone, she asked for a number in Scotland and then booked a personal call to Kit Vanston.

Vivien hummed to herself as she walked back to the château from Arbon, feeling pleased with the day's events. She had hoped for more; but at least there was some chance that she would be able to track down her daughter. She was so deep in thought, wondering what Yvette would be like, that she did not see Gordon waiting for her by the back entrance.

'What the hell were you playing at?' he shouted. 'Going

off like that! You had clear instructions not to leave Zoe alone.'

'Do you mean she went ahead and took it?' Vivien asked. 'Is she OK?'

'Just about. No thanks to you!'

Vivien looked troubled. 'I was sure she would wait. I'd told her . . .'

'I told *you* to get there. You disobeyed orders. Why?'

Vivien told Gordon some story about having a previous rendezvous with a man she knew from her wine-trading days, who might be useful to them. He looked at her in disbelief and asked her when she had arranged the meeting; she paused for a moment and then said two days previously.

This information only intensified Gordon's anger.

'So when I gave you your orders, you already knew you meant to disobey them? Yet you said nothing.'

'We'd already arranged to meet. So I was wrong. What is all this?'

Gordon remained silent for a moment and then looked sharply at Vivien. 'Why did you go to the Town Hall a couple of weeks back?'

She tried to hide her surprise. 'André's orders, to make a contact. It didn't work out.'

Looking at Gordon's brooding face, she suddenly became equally angry.

'I do what André says,' she insisted. 'No one's told me to obey you. What makes you think you've some God-given right to act the big boots? Just because you're a bloke?'

Gordon smiled briefly. 'London has cleared it. I'm the leader of this circuit now.'

Vivien felt her heart sink as he continued. 'André is finished here. They've worked out an escape route via

Spain. And if we weren't in such straits, I'd send you back with him. He's off tomorrow; you'll go with him on the bus as far as Limogne. I'll give you full instructions.' He looked hard at her. 'Can I rely on you to carry them out?'

Vivien stared back at him and replied with heavy irony in an American drawl, 'OK, boss!'

As she walked up the drive to the château, she felt sick. All pleasure at her own discovery had disappeared with the news about Emily. The news that she would have to obey Gordon was hard to take, as well.

Vivien made an excuse to Juliette and set off back to the town. A tight-lipped Marie told her where she could find Emily, and for the second time that day, she found that she had to visit a church.

Emily was kneeling in front of a madonna in a small side chapel. She seemed to have spent a small fortune on candles. She was deep in prayer, her knuckles white from the intense pressure with which she clasped them. A few tears rolled slowly down her face.

Sitting some distance away, Vivien waited for Emily to finish praying. Watching the girl, she felt increasingly upset and guilty about having let her down. When Emily finally stood up, Vivien darted up the side aisle and grasped her arm. The young girl put her arms round Vivien and the two embraced.

Vivien supported Emily as they walked out of the church into the still, dusk air. She knew her excuses sounded pat and unconvincing, as Emily desperately tried to sound unconcerned. Now was not the time to share her secret with the girl.

The two women sat down side by side on a wooden bench overlooking neat rows of tombs, each surrounded by a little border of marble chippings and a small metal rail.

Vivien handed Emily a handkerchief and told her to have a good blow.

'I can't stop thinking about my parents,' Emily sighed.

'They'll understand,' said Vivien, trying to be comforting.

Emily laughed, slightly hysterically.

'If they could know where you are – the work you're doing,' continued Vivien, 'they'd be so proud.'

Emily burst into tears. 'I can never tell them what I did.'

'Never's too big a word for it. One day, if you want to, you'll be able to tell them . . . all of it.'

Emily shook her head. 'My mother would disown me,' she said sadly.

Vivien persisted. 'She'd understand – and your father.'

'He's always so busy with his patients . . . and my brothers and sisters.'

Vivien tried to divert her friend.

'My old dad ran a little shop. Best cod and chips in town. At school I simply stank of fat. I had their total attention. Believe me, it isn't so great.'

'I've let them down,' sobbed Emily.

'No, you've done what you had to do.'

'I keep having nightmares about eternal hellfire and all that.'

'It was an accident, Zoe – something that was never meant to happen. And now it's over, like a bad dream.'

Emily looked along the rows of graves and up to the church and sighed sadly.

'I don't think so.'

'But you've just confessed,' said Vivien, guessing the purpose of Emily's visit to the church. 'So it's all forgiven now.'

'You don't understand,' explained Emily. 'There was no forgiveness. No absolution. It was murder, you see, and you can't run away from that.'

Liz's briefing from Faith was carried out professionally, but there was an undercurrent of tension. Neither woman was quite sure what the other was thinking as Faith gave Liz her cover story and her instructions on how to blow up the German radio transmitter in Area 7.

At the end, Liz nodded dully.

'Is there anything else I can do for you?' Faith asked.

Liz thought back to the briefing she had had before being sent out with Matty. Then, she had asked Faith to post some prewritten postcards to Vicky.

'I've called my mother,' said Liz. 'We talked a lot. Perhaps you could contact her from time to time?'

'Yes,' agreed Faith. 'And Vicky – do you have a message for her?'

There was a long pause before Liz replied, 'I've decided it's better if Vicky forgets me.'

Faith looked with surprise at her colleague and friend. 'You don't have to give her up,' she said.

'Laurence has it all worked out. I think it will be for the best.'

'I hope you're right,' sighed Faith. Liz's attitude only confirmed the misgivings she already felt about the wisdom of sending her over to France.

Liz leaned forward. 'I do have to go, Faith. You know how desperate the situation is over there.' Her mind went to Kit. 'Anyway, there's nothing for me here. Not now.'

They went over Liz's new identity once more and then Liz cleared her desk.

She said good-night to the porter more warmly than

usual; she had a little mental list of goodbyes to say before her departure. Deep in thought as she walked through the swing doors of Parkgrove Mansions, she did not notice the man hanging about outside, but set off up the road, walking briskly towards the underground station.

As the man hurried after her and called out her name; Liz stopped in her tracks and turned around. Instantaneously, her face lit up.

'Kit!' she said. 'What are you doing here?'

He took her by the arm and said urgently, 'We've got to talk.'

As they walked along, he explained how Faith had telephoned him and told him that Liz's marriage was over.

'Why didn't *you* call me?' he asked.

'I wasn't sure how you felt now. But it couldn't have made any difference to my decision. You know I'm flying out tonight?'

'I know you volunteered, yes.' Kit sounded quiet but determined. 'You're not to go.'

They stopped walking and looked at each other.

'A lot has been going wrong in Area 7,' said Liz.

'I realize they're pretty desperate.'

'They need me; that's why I'm going.'

'You're not going!' Kit exclaimed. 'For God's sake, I'm not going through all that again: not knowing if you're dead or alive. I'll replace you; Cad will agree to it and I can leave . . .'

Liz was furious.

'How dare you?' she shouted. 'How dare you order me about? You're not even asking me.'

They stood glaring at each other.

'All right, I'm asking you,' he said awkwardly.

'The plane leaves tonight, and I'll be on it. They need me. I do have some value, in the field at least.'

Kit stared at her in shock and then turned away.

'That's that then,' he mumbled.

Liz grabbed hold of his arm as he tried to walk away.

'Can't you wish me luck?' she pleaded.

'No, damn it!' said Kit. 'I can't!'

He strode off down the road leaving Liz staring after him, her feelings in turmoil.

Vivien was secretly delighted to see Gordon's resentment at the news that André was to be replaced so quickly.

'Just as I was getting things into some sort of order,' grumbled Gordon.

'Yes,' said Vivien, hoping that her insincerity was not too apparent. 'Still, I'm sure it's all for the best.'

For old times' sake, Vivien accompanied Colin on the first stage of his long journey up through the hills and over the Pyrenees to safety. His nerves were shot to pieces. Vivien somehow doubted he would make the journey home and – if he did – whether he would ever fully recover.

'Good luck,' she said, and kissed him.

Colin merely nodded silently.

'Say hello to England for us,' added Vivien lightly.

But Colin was already trudging away and didn't seem to have heard.

Faith drove Liz to the airfield. Within the last few hours, Liz's appearance had been completely altered; her hair had been cut in a French style and her clothes too were in keeping with her new identity. The one thing that had not changed was her expression of sadness.

She noticed Faith looking at her with concern.

'Don't worry, Faith,' she said with more confidence than she really felt. 'I'll be back.'

Fortunately, weather conditions were favourable and the moon shone down on the airstrip as Liz and Faith said their farewells in the shadow of the Halifax bomber. They kissed each other, then Liz climbed up inside the plane and disappeared, leaving Faith to wonder if she would ever see her again.

Gordon made the most of his last minutes in command, ordering around the reception committee consisting of Emily, Josef, Louis and two other Frenchmen. He explained to Emily with ill-disguised impatience the procedure of setting out the lights in an L-shaped pattern to mark the target area and lighting them only when one could hear the sound of the plane's engine approaching.

Emily was still weak and tired enough to be grateful when he offered to position the last of the lights for her: less pleased when he muttered something about it being 'man's work, really'.

Finally, after a long wait, the distant sound of an approaching Halifax was heard. Shortly afterwards, they looked up to see a number of parachutes drifting down to the ground.

The reception committee ran forward out of the trees to collect the containers which had been dropped; Gordon and Emily went to greet their new leader, who landed perfectly. Gordon stopped in his tracks as the approaching figure took off her helmet and shook out her hair.

'What the ruddy hell are they thinking of?' he muttered to himself, but not quietly enough.

Liz turned and greeted him coolly. 'Hello, Gaspard.'

More warmly, she turned to Emily. 'Hello, Zoe.'

'It's you!' said Emily, remembering Liz from those training days which now seemed so long ago.

Before she could say any more, Liz introduced herself.

'I'm Colette now. I'm your new leader.'

This time Gordon did not bother to conceal his outrage.

'You're *what?*'

'Right. Let's go,' said Liz briskly, and started to organize the loading of the containers into the truck.

CHAPTER 4

Liz observed Gordon's sour expression as she poured him a glass of wine. If you can't swallow your pride, she thought, you can at least drink some wine.

'Coming to France does have some compensations,' she smiled, indicating the bottle.

'I've always preferred whisky,' said Gordon stiffly.

They sat facing each other across the kitchen table in Liz's safe house. Gordon soon forgot his animosity, however, as he studied the RAF aerial photographs which Liz had brought with her. They gave a good general idea of the layout of the German transmitting station; it consisted of a number of huts with aerials, surrounded by a tall fence with two gates. He studied the photographs intently and then told Liz his requirements.

'I need a diagram of the masts: width of cables, height of the base. They have to be accurate.'

'I'll get one,' Liz assured him. 'So if we blow up just one aerial, they can't transmit?'

'Aye,' Gordon nodded. 'But getting into the compound – that's the problem.'

Liz was already ahead of the game; she had sent out Vivien first thing that morning to take a look at the installation.

'Solange is doing a recce. If it's essential, she may be able to work from inside.'

Gordon looked at Liz shrewdly. 'It's a big job.'

'I'll be working with you, of course, placing the charges.'

Gordon put the photographs down on the table and looked at her with open scepticism.

'And for back-up, we'll have to rely on French help,' she continued. 'What are they like?'

'Josef's lot? Untrained, undisciplined. André never really got down to it. I was going to start giving them basics on explosives.'

Liz leaned forward and looked at him keenly.

'There's a lot you can tell me, Gaspard.'

'Such as?' He pretended not to know what she was getting at.

'The others. I know what Zoe went through. Has she got over it, do you think?'

'You'll have to ask her yourself. A good reliable worker, that girl.'

'And Solange?'

There was a slight pause whilst Gordon considered his reply and his silence only confirmed Liz's own misgivings.

'She does her job,' he said finally.

'But?'

'You know what I'm driving at.'

'Why not say?'

Liz got up from the table, went to the window and looked out for a few moments. Then she turned round and folded her arms.

'I need to know *everything* you can tell me. I'm worried about security in this area. That Milicienne who was shot – why were they looking for a British agent? Or did they think André was French? And how did they know about his safe house?'

Gordon shrugged his shoulders. 'I've no idea,' he grunted.

'Was he being followed?' persisted Liz.

Gordon shrugged again.

'You think there's an informer?'

'None of us has been picked up.'

'Not yet,' said Liz. 'But André very nearly was.'

Gordon looked glum and shook his head. He felt the same disquiet as she did, but there was nothing specific that he could pinpoint.

Vivien arrived not long after Gordon had left, and likewise could shed no light on why Colin had been followed. Liz gave instructions to her courier.

'I'm changing all routines and tightening up security. The dead-letter drops will all be replaced – so will the passwords.'

'A new broom,' smiled Vivien. 'I'm sure you're right.'

'There'll be no contact between people in this circuit, except through me. You'll come here for your instructions.'

Vivien looked round the kitchen approvingly.

'Good-oh! This is rather a jolly place. Were you dying to come out, or did they have to twist your arm?'

'I came out because I'm needed,' replied Liz coolly.

'Well, it's put Gaspard's nose right out of joint,' laughed Vivien.

Liz decided to change the subject. 'You were with Zoe, when she had the miscarriage?'

'Yes,' said Vivien. 'It was tough, but she's OK now.'

'Are you sure?' Something in Vivien's voice made Liz suspicious.

'Mmm. Oh, she's loaded with Catholic guilt, but I've

given her a good talking-to. I mean, devils with forks and flames and stuff: it's a bit old hat!'

Liz couldn't help smiling at Vivien's cynicism.

'Oh, I nearly forgot,' said Vivien, lifting up her skirt and removing a folded peice of paper from the hem.

Liz unfolded the paper and was surprised to see a detailed sketch of the German transmitting station. Vivien leaned forward with excitement as she described what she had seen.

'The fence round the compound is no good to us. Gaspard will have to get through the side gate – but it's locked and barred from the inside.'

'This will be very useful,' acknowledged Liz. "But weren't you taking a big risk by getting in so close?'

'Oh well,' Vivien laughed, 'it's *my* neck.'

'We're a team, Solange,' Liz reminded her, 'and you're the link that bind's us together. If you go, we all go. You must understand.'

'Well, blow me! I thought you'd be pleased!' Vivien exclaimed.

All the old antagonism between the two women was suddenly rekindled and Vivien walked back to the château in high dudgeon. She had not been spoken to like that since her schooldays.

Liz waited for ten mintues after Vivien had left before setting out to visit Emily. Marie looked at her with distrust when she asked to see the girl, who was resting upstairs in her bedroom.

'I expect you know what happened,' said Marie as they waited for Emily to come downstairs. 'Zoe needs a rest.'

Emily came into the kitchen and stood next to Marie, who put her arm round her. Liz noticed with some concern the mutual warmth and affection which the women obviously felt. It could be dangerous for two people to get too fond of each other, especially when one was a foreign agent. Marie squeezed Emily's shoulder and went back into the shop, leaving the two Englishwomen to talk alone.

'Marie worries too much,' said Emily.

'You seem very fond of each other?'

'Oh, not really,' replied Emily unconvincingly. 'But I don't know what I'd do without them at the moment.'

'You don't ever transmit from here?' asked Liz.

'No, of course not.' Emily looked at Liz in surprise. 'It's a different place each time. I never bring my set back, either.'

She brought bowls of coffee over from the stove and they sat down at the table.

'I won't be contacting you directly again.' said Liz. 'It'll always be through Solange or one of the new drops. You got my message?'

Emily nodded.

'Good. There's another for your next sked. We've got a lot more information about our target.' Liz paused for a moment and then ploughed on. 'I came here because I need to know how you are – really.'

Liz looked at the pretty, wan face, imagining how Vicky might look in a few years. She hoped that her daughter would never have to go through a similar experience.

'Oh, I'm fine,' Emily protested. 'But there is one thing. . . .'

'What's that?' Liz asked.

'My boy-friend . . . it was his baby. Does he know anything about it?'

Liz understood what Emily was trying to say.

'You didn't want us to tell him.'

'When you were out here the first time,' said Emily hesitantly, 'did you change a lot?'

When Liz left the Ferrier's shop, she checked the street outside but failed to notice the curtains moving in a neighbouring house. As she walked up the road, she spotted a familiar figure coming towards her, wheeling a perambulator. Immediately she crossed over to the other side and waited round the corner.

Emily was surprised by Vivien's arrival in the shop. Quickly, Marie ushered them both through to Leon's work-room at the back and fetched some wine for the unexpected visitor. Emily also found it hard to understand Vivien's mood; it was almost as if she had something to celebrate. While Emily waited for Vivien to come to the point, she played with the baby and felt a little pang at what she had lost.

'When this bloody war is over,' said Vivien, seeing Emily's sadness, 'you'll go home and marry your nice bloke and have a horde of kids.'

She raised her glass in a kind of salute.

'You didn't, though,' observed Emily glumly.

'*I* didn't. One hell of a huge mistake, allowing Yvette's adoption.'

The women looked at each other.

'Yvette? Was that what you called her?' asked Emily.

'Yes.'

'A French name.' Emily thought for a moment and then looked at Vivien. 'She's over here, isn't she, Solange?'

Vivien gave a little laugh.

'I wanted you to guess! Too many secrets, for too long!' She paused for a moment. 'I had her when I was working over here, a long time ago.'

'Where does she live now?'

This turned out to be the news that Vivien wished to share with her friend. After she had got back to the château from visiting Liz, she had telephoned Father Giraud who had tracked down the Moreaus' address for her.

'In Toulouse,' Vivien said excitedly. 'Not very far away! The couple who adopted her, they disappeared in all the chaos. The local priest has been helping.'

Emily looked worried. 'You haven't been trying to trace her?'

'More than that. After all these years, I know exactly where she is and I'm going to see her, Zoe!'

Emily looked even more worried. 'Is that wise? You could blow your cover.'

'I've *got* to know if she's OK,' Vivien said intensely. 'If things turned out all right for her . . . and maybe. . . . Well, just to see her.'

Emily thought for a while and then looked hard at Vivien.

'Is that why you volunteered? And came out here?'

'No, don't think that,' said Vivien hurriedly. 'But of course they did come into it – Yvette and Johnny.'

This time, it was her turn to stare hard at Emily. 'You're not to breathe a word to anyone. Promise?'

'I can't do that,' Emily said. 'My whole life at the moment is full of lies.'

'But I only told you because I thought I could trust you!' Vivien cried. 'You won't tell, will you?'

Emily slowly shook her head.

'Ever!' insisted Vivien. 'Do you promise?'

'OK. OK. I promise.' Emily sighed. 'But for heaven's sake, be careful!'

Vivien laughed her harsh laugh.

'Oh, I'm one of life's survivors. But I might need you to cover for me.'

'But I couldn't . . .'

Vivien didn't let her finish.

'Doesn't matter. I was only thinking of Colette. "Yes, ma'am. No, ma'am." Bloody paragon!'

Dusk was beginning to fall as Vivien left the shop and started to push the pram up the street. She had not told Juliette that she was going out, and now she was in a hurry to get back to the château. Vivien was so absorbed in planning her trip to see Yvette that she did not notice that she was being followed. All at once a hand reached out and touched her shoulder and she swung round in fear.

Her shock turned to relief when she saw it was Liz – who was, however, plainly angry. She ordered Vivien to walk on and pretend that they were old friends chatting. When they reached the town square, Liz made her sit down under one of the columns of the covered market-place.

Vivien tried to think up a plausible excuse for visiting Emily, but Liz was having none of it.

'What *were* you doing?' she insisted on knowing.

'Taking a message to Zoe.'

'I didn't give you any message.'

'I wanted to make sure she knew about the letter drops.'

'That is not your job, Solange,' said Liz pointedly.

'The truth is, I've had to keep an eye on her. I thought you'd have wanted that?'

'You were in there for half an hour.'

'And what were you doing, lurking around?' asked Vivien incredulously. 'Trying to catch me out, or what?'

'And then you didn't even notice you were being trailed. Whatever were you thinking of?'

The two women looked stonyfaced as a peasant woman wandered by with the remains of the wares she had been selling in the market.

'There was no need to sneak after me like that! Frightened the life out of me!'

'It could have been the Gestapo! I don't know what's been going on here. You seem to think you can come and go exactly as you please.'

'I showed a bit of initiative, that's all!' Vivien protested.

'Then don't!' said Liz through clenched teeth. 'Let me spell it out. From now on, you go only *where* I say, *when* I say. Is that clear?'

The two women glared at each other.

The following day, Liz went out with Josef checking the various places where guns and ammunition had been stored. She was concerned to discover that he knew the location of every single stache, stressing the need that none of them should know the complete picture in case they fell into German hands.

Josef acknowledged that tight security was necessary, but grumbled that he was much more concerned about getting arms and sabotage training for his men. Liz was able to assure him that Gaspard would start training immediately.

'Not before time!' exclaimed Josef. 'Gaspard will need my help on the transmitter operation.'

'No, I'll be going in with him,' said Liz.

Josef looked at her with astonishment. 'You?'

'I'm the area leader. You and one of your men will lead two back-ups to get us away.'

She paused for a moment while he digested what she had just said, then continued, 'Tell me about your inside contact.'

'Jeanne? What do you want to know?'

'How much does she know?'

'About the plans for the raid – just about everything.' Liz looked disapproving as he continued, 'She's been planted there for some time, waiting for you lot to sort yourselves out.'

Biting back a sharp remark, Liz asked what Jeanne knew about the British agents.

'Nothing,' said Josef. 'And Jeanne is absolutely reliable – always has been.'

Liz thought over what Josef had said and told him her requirements for the operation to succeed: a copy of the key to the side gate and an accurate diagram of the aerial masts, the base and cables.

'I'll get a message to her,' promised Josef.

'And she must brief Solange on her cover,' Liz added.

Vivien found Jeanne working at the bottom of her garden. She was busy washing clothes in the river while her small son tried to skim stones across the water.

'I think you may have my husband's shirt,' Vivien said. 'A blue one with long sleeves.'

Jeanne – a stout, red-faced woman – looked older than she really was because of her hard life as a washer-woman. She wiped her chapped hands on her apron and told the lad to hang up the laundry and then go away to play.

'Solange?' Jeanne turned to Vivien.

'Yes, you're Jeanne,' said Vivien, appraising the Frenchwoman. They both liked what they saw; in fact, they were very similar women: both strong and vivacious.

Jeanne started to explain to Vivien the nature of her cover.

'You will be bringing fresh produce for the farms, two nights a week – and helping me with the laundry.'

'Sound's glamorous,' laughed Vivien. 'What's my cover?'

Jeanne told Vivien that she would be impersonating a woman who had disappeared a few months before. She produced a small, tatty photo from her pocket and passed it to Vivien, who studied it intently. She was to be called Victoire Lacoste; born in Toulouse in 1903. Her husband, a vineyard worker, had died of pneumonia before the war, and her daughter had been killed the previous year.

'I can tell you every detail you might need,' said Jeanne.

'She's somebody you know?' Vivien asked.

'Yes. They'll interview you. I don't know,' the woman looked closely at Vivien. 'You don't look right. And if they . . .'

'Oh,' said Vivien with her usual confidence, 'don't worry. It'll be a piece of cake.'

Back at the château, the transformation from Vivien into Victoire was extraordinary. Juliette helped to dye her hair and restyle it; the Frenchwoman gave Vivien some peasant women's clothes which she had been saving for rags.

Vivien peered at her reflection in the mirror as she pushed the little round wire spectacles up her nose. Meanwhile Juliette stood back and admired her handiwork. Her old friend was no longer recognizable; it would be difficult to spot the difference between Vivien and the faded snapshop. For a moment, she saw a tiny flash of panic cross Vivien's face.

'Aren't you afraid?' Juliette asked.

Vivien smiled wryly, turned to her friend and confided that she was absolutely terrified.

The first test of Vivien's new identity was at the interview for the job in the transmitting station. She stood in front of the desk, clutching her handbag nervously in front of her.

The German doing the interviewing – Voller – rifled through a file of documents and gave a cursory glance at the ID card which Vivien handed him. Then he asked her why she wanted the job.

Vivien looked down at her scuffed lace-up shoes and then up at the officer.

'I need to live,' she said with a bitter tone in her voice.

'Not every Frenchwoman would choose to work here.'

She continued as if she had not grasped what he had just said. 'I've an arrangement with a farm. That's how I can supply you. I only work in the season.'

'And you travel round the vineyards?'

'Taking produce to the workers.'

'Then you will know Monsieur Dupont and his family?'

Vivien's heart sank as she floundered for a moment, then she realized what to do: play ignorant.

'M'sieur Dupont?' she asked.

Voller looked at her sharply.

'Which one do you mean?' explained Vivien. 'It's a common enough name.'

'They own Château Mavrois,' explained the officer, looking at her carefully.

Vivien snorted. 'Oh, them! I never deal with owners. What would they want with me?'

'They were arrested last week. I thought everyone knew about it.'

'I've nobody to tell me such news.'

'No friends?'

'I have no friends, not since my daughter's death.'

'So you are not afraid of being unpopular?'

'Me?' Vivien gave a bitter little laugh, acting away as she had never had much chance to do in her professional career.

Voller returned to the file of papers and drew one out of the pile. 'Your daughter was killed last year, I see?'

Vivien began to talk animatedly.

'She was sleeping in her bed when the British murdered her! I have her picture. Here, look.' She started to open the locket which was hanging round her neck. 'She was only ten years old!'

The officer gestured to Vivien to put the locket away and she did so slowly, first taking a long look at the picture inside it.

'And your house was destroyed?'

'They said the bomb was meant for a factory.' Vivien spoke very quietly; she was still very tense, but the performance was beginning to take over and part of her almost believed she was Victoire.

The officer replaced the papers in the folder and closed it. Then he looked up at Vivien and studied her briefly.

'The laundress says that she could do with some help.'

'I can do that!' Vivien hoped she did not sound too eager.

'Your rate of pay will be the same as hers. And the mess officer will give orders for each delivery.'

Voller indicated with his head that the interview was

over. Vivien muttered a short thank-you and walked out of the room. She had to concentrate very hard so as not to skip out of the radio station.

Once she had been ushered out of the side gate and had cycled some way up the road, however, she burst into song. She pedalled like mad, wishing to share her success with Emily.

As Vivien cycled away, Jeanne was at work inside the transmitting station, wheeling the laundry trolley along the corridor in the main block. She paused for a moment as a soldier came out of the guards' room, watching him walk up the corridor out of sight. Waiting a few moments to make sure that he had gone, Jeanne checked that the guards' room was empty and scuttled inside.

Hurriedly, she reached up to the row of hooks with keys hanging from them and looking along the row, found the key to the side gate. She produced a tin of wax polish from her apron pocket, and opened it so that she could take an impression.

Jeanne's heart pounded as she finished the job and replaced the key on its hook. Slipping the tin of polish back into her pocket, she sighed with relief and turned towards the door. She froze in terror as she saw a German guard standing in the open doorway. He had observed everything that she had done.

Vivien re-enacted her star performance for Emily as they sat in the Ferriers' kitchen. Emily found herself completely involved in Vivien's account, but suddenly clapped her hand to her mouth in realization.

'You shouldn't be telling me all this!' she cried out.

'Oh, phooey!' exclaimed Vivien. 'They hired me. It's all on for the raid. That's why . . . '

Before Vivien could tell Emily about her plans, the young girl interrupted her. 'And you shouldn't have come here. What would Colette say?'

Vivien pulled a face. 'Our "Head Girl" is the problem. I've got to go into Toulouse tomorrow to see Yvette.'

Emily looked at her in dismay.

'Why tomorrow, Solange? We'll get the go-ahead on the BBC any day now.'

'That's why. After the raid I'll have to lie very low.' She paused for a moment. 'Besides, supposing something went wrong?'

She registered Emily's look of concern, but carried on regardless. 'It has to be tomorrow. But there's "Big-boots" to contend with. Could you spin a yarn if necessary?'

'You mean lie to her about where you are?'

'Just this once for me. It's the only chance I'll have to see my daughter.'

There was a moment's silence between the two women and then, much against her better judgment, Emily nodded her head.

'All right,' she said tentatively.

Vivien jumped up from her chair and hugged her friend. 'Bless you!' She noticed the worried expression on Emily's face. 'It's only if she comes snooping round.'

'You must get back. It'll be curfew soon,' Emily reminded her.

Vivien took a dreary headscarf from her basket, tied it round her head and adjusted her spectacles. Then she picked up her basket and waved a cheery goodbye to Emily.

'OK. Thanks a million, Zoe.'

Emily watched Vivien leave and sat still for a moment, thinking anxiously. Vivien's behaviour was such that she almost seemed to be deliberately tempting fate.

Gradually, Liz set about the task of winning Gordon's confidence. Together they planned the attack on the transmitting station. Jeanne's early work in providing the team with measurements of the aerial mast and its supports proved invaluable. Gordon explained to Liz where the charges would need to be set, in order to blow up the aerial. She was pleasantly surprised at his reaction when she repeated that she would be going in with him.

'Reckon I could do worse,' he said grudgingly.

Liz smiled at him. This was evidently the nearest Gordon ever got to uttering a compliment. He looked at Liz shrewdly, as if he were about to take her into his confidence.

'There's one thing I'd like to know,' he said hesitantly. 'How much do we have to rely on Solange?'

Liz asked him what he meant and Gordon told her about Vivien's less than convincing explanation of her visit to the Town Hall.

'She told me it was on André's orders . . . to make a contact. He isn't here to say if it's true or not.'

'Did you believe Solange?' asked Liz, her suspicions beginning to mount.

'At the time. But I've thought about it since – it just doesn't make sense.' Gordon paused. 'Unless the contact was on the other side.'

Back at the château, Vivien resumed her normal appearance. She was standing in the hall, putting her lipstick on, when Juliette came through with the baby in her arms and looked at her admiringly.

'If I didn't know it was all work, I'd think it was some other kind of rendezvous,' she said, laughing.

'No such luck!' Vivien pulled a face.

'You look radiant.'

Vivien kissed her friend and the baby. Then she strode down the corridor to the front door. She stood for a moment at the entrance and called back to Juliette that she would be home late; then pirouetted and swept out of the house.

Vivien could hardly control the excitement bubbling up inside her. She wondered whether the other passengers on the bus could guess that something special was going to happen to her. She was so wrapped up in her own thoughts that she did not notice when the bus passed Liz cycling in the direction of the château. The whole of the journey to Toulouse passed in a dream.

Rue Levallier was not difficult to find; it was a street of modest houses not far from the bus station. Vivien stood outside No. 24 and eyed it carefully. Her initial reaction did not fill her with hope; it seemed to be the opposite of everything that was her style – box-like house, with the front windows completely curtained off from the street. To Vivien it reeked of stodgy bourgeois domesticity.

'Don't judge by appearances,' she said to herself. Eventually, she summoned up enough courage to ring the door-bell.

A small ordinary-looking woman in her late fifties opened the door.

'Marguerite Moreau?' Vivien asked.

'What can I do for you?' responded the woman in a harsh voice.

Biting back her disappointment, Vivien switched on her charm and told Marguerite the cover story which she had concocted. She pretended to be a representative of a charity recruiting support to send comforts to French prisoners in Germany.

Marguerite asked Vivien to come in to the small, formal front room. As they both sat on hard straight-backed chairs, Vivien took in the decor with mounting horror: a large ugly cabinet was crammed full of every sort of religious knick-knack.

Marguerite listened intently to what Vivien had to say. 'I've heard about this,' she said, looking interested. 'To write them letters?'

'Yes, young pen pals or to knit some socks. They're having an awful time out there. And you've got a daughter aged nineteen . . . Yvette?'

'You know about Yvette?' Marguerite looked puzzled.

'Our charity has information from the lycée.'

Before Vivien could continue, the front door banged shut and a young girl's voice called out: 'Maman?'

Marguerite called the girl into the front room and as she entered Vivien looked at her intently. She was a pretty child, but in a very conventional way. Vivien felt disappointment welling up within her.

'Chérie! You are so late!'

Marguerite chided the girl fondly. Clearly she doted on her.

'I am sorry, Maman,' The girl kissed her mother with equal affection.

Marguerite introduced Vivien. 'This lady has come to talk about the prisoners of war.'

'Oh. Pleased to meet you,' the girl said politely.

'Hello.' Vivien tried to speak normally. 'Are you Yvette?'

The girl laughed scornfully and Marguerite rushed into explain.

'This is my daughter Madeleine.' Vivien felt a sense of relief. 'I am sure *she* will help the prisoners.'

'And Yvette will she be home soon?'

Marguerite's mouth tightened. 'I'm afraid not.'

Madeleine stood with her arm around her mother's shoulder. 'Yvette doesn't live with us any more,' the young girl said primly.

Vivien looked at the two women gazing at her with hostility and decided to be frank.

'I'm sorry. You see . . . I am Yvette's mother.'

There was a long pause as Marguerite studied Vivien's face intently. 'I can see it now; you have the same eyes.'

Vivien's face lit up with pleasure. 'Do I?'

'Everyone says that Madeleine takes after me,' said Marguerite.

'You're very alike,' Vivien assured her.

Marguerite and Madeleine smiled back.

'Do you have a photo of Yvette?' Vivien asked, as the atmosphere thawed.

'Somewhere. Henri and I didn't know when we adopted her that we'd soon have a baby daughter of our own; it was an unexpected blessing.'

'You say she left home last year?'

'I don't know where she is now.'

Marguerite rose from her chair and started searching through her bureau. From the back of a drawer she pulled out a photo of Yvette.

'Do you live near Toulouse?' Marguerite asked Vivien.

'I was married to a man in the wine trade,' said Vivien evasively. 'I live not too far away.'

Marguerite gave her the photograph, which she studied eagerly.

'Why didn't you contact us before, if Yvette was on your mind?' asked Marguerite.

'It was difficult with my husband – and I thought everything was going well.'

'Well, Madame, I did my best. Somehow she just never fitted in.'

Madeleine leapt in to defend her mother.

'Yvette treated my mother very badly. Mother has a weak heart now, I think from all the worry and arguments.'

'Hush, Madeleine!'

'Have you really no idea where she is?' pressed Vivien.

'She went off with a gang of friends – not good types, you understand?'

Vivien leaned forward. 'I need to see her. Will you help me?'

Marguerite considered Vivien's request.

'I suppose . . . Pierre's mother will have the address.'

Vivien sat back in her chair.

'Thank you,' she said gratefully.

Liz spent the day finalizing plans for the raid. As dawn broke, she and Gordon prepared the plastic explosive charges. Gordon was in good spirits, humming away to himself as he removed the explosives from their hiding-place in an underground wine cellar. Carefully, he unwrapped the greaseproof paper.

'Take a pound of marzipan,' he murmured happily as he cut the explosive. He did not pick up on Liz's pensive mood as they moulded it into open-ended yellow sausages which would fit round the thick cables attached to the aerial.

'All set for tomorrow, then?' he asked, looking across at her.

'Yes. We'll meet by the forest track.'

'Do we have both getaway vehicles?'

'As planned.' Liz nodded. 'Josef will provide the decoy if it's needed. There's just one thing . . .'

Gordon now registered the worry in Liz's voice.

'Zoe. I'm including her in the back-up with the French.'

Gordon looked at Liz in surprise. 'Is that wise? Risking our pianist.'

'There's nobody else and at least she can be trusted.'

'Well, you're the boss,' Gordon said, sounding dubious.

'Did you decide on the time pencils?'

'One hour.'

'Will that be enough time for everybody?'

'Ah, aye. To melt away before the big bang.' He looked at Liz. 'Something's on your mind?'

'It's Solange. She disappeared yesterday.'

Gordon listened as Liz described her trip to the château, where Juliette had told her of Vivien's visit to Toulouse.

'Why would she do that?' Liz asked.

'It's not the first time,' replied Gordon.

'What do you mean?'

'When young Zoe was in trouble, Solange went against my orders and left her on her own.'

Liz looked shocked. 'But that's unforgivable!' she exclaimed angrily.

'There was no harm done, as it turned out.' Gordon tried to play the incident down.

The pair sat on the floor of the cellar, leaned back against the large wooden vats and pondered the situation. Finally Liz broke the silence.

'I wonder if it's wise to go ahead tomorrow.'

Gordon looked at her anxiously. He was fed up with doing nothing and desperately wanted to see some action.

'Ah, now,' he said, trying to placate Liz. 'She's probably just taking some time off – against the rules, but there it is.'

Liz looked unconvinced.

'What's our go-ahead message?' Gordon asked, to rouse her from her reverie.

'"Aunt Doreen is taking the boys to lunch."'

Gordon hooted with laughter.

'And what's on the menu?' He held up two of the charges they had prepared. 'Bangers, is it?'

Liz looked at him in surprise. It seemed the dour Scot had a lighter side, after all.

Vivien shut the door behind her and walked across to Liz.

'Got your message,' she said, sauntering into Liz's apartment. 'Last briefing for tomorrow night?'

Liz had had very little sleep from worrying and was in no mood for flippancy. She stood up straight against the window so that all that Vivien could see was her dark outline silhouetted against the sky.

'Where were you yesterday?' she demanded.

Vivien stood still, looking at Liz, and finally replied, 'I went out.' Then, after an uncomfortable pause, she decided to elucidate. 'Toulouse for the day. Bit of light relief. You hadn't given me any orders.'

'Sit down!' snapped Liz.

Vivien sat down on a small upright chair with a wicker seat and crossed her legs nonchalantly, staring up at Liz with an insolent expression on her face.

'You have excellent recall.' Liz spoke very slowly. 'It's one of the reasons you were chosen.'

'OK. I know you said . . .'

'To go only *where* I said, *when* I said. You disobeyed orders. Why?'

'I needed a break. I had to get away.' Vivien sounded unconvincing.

'And that's more important than the job you're here to do?' demanded Liz. 'There's something about you I'm not sure I can trust.'

That was too much for Vivien. She leapt up and screamed in Liz's face, 'Just for one day I did what I damn well pleased!'

'You know the rules,' Liz replied icily.

Vivien looked at her with deep loathing. This English rose certainly had some vicious thorns, she thought.

'You've never liked me, have you?' she accused.

Liz maintained her lofty manner. 'This isn't personal,' she replied.

'No?' Vivien shouted belligerently.

'You have been warned.' For the first time, Liz sounded personally aggressive. 'One more idiotic foolish trick and you'll be on the first plane back home.'

'I'm a damn good courier and you can't afford to lose me,' Vivien asserted. 'And what about tomorrow night? You'll never do it without me.'

'I can cancel it,' Liz said quietly.

Vivien looked at her, appalled. Was this a serious suggestion?

'No, Colette,' she pleaded 'You can't afford to. It's too important.'

'What I can't afford is to risk everybody.'

Looking at Liz's stern face, Vivien decided the best approach was to eat humble pie.

'Look, I'm sorry,' she said, using all her acting skill.

'I've always been straight with you. So I was wrong to take a day off. I should've asked you first, somehow.'

Liz looked at her, unsure how to take this change of tack.

'They need this operation to succeed,' Vivien pressed on imploringly. 'You need me in there. I swear I'll do exactly what you say.'

Liz thought rapidly and decided that she had to trust Vivien. Probably she was just a very undisciplined woman who had no evil intent. Going over to the sofa, she unfastened one of the cushion-covers and pulled out an RAF aerial photograph of the radio transmitting station. Then she sat down on the sofa and indicated that Vivien join her.

'You'll have to memorize the exterior layout,' Liz said.

Relieved, Vivien concentrated hard on the picture.

'Jeanne will give you the key. And she'll tell you when. Your job is to signal, then let in Gaspard and me – here, through the side gate into the compound.'

Vivien stared hard at the photo for a few minutes, then looked up and nodded.

'I've got it. And Jeanne?'

'She'll be taking care of the guards at the front gate,' Liz replied.

She indicated that the session was at an end and watched Vivien leave the room. Liz returned to the window and hit her fist angrily against the pane of glass. Why, oh why, didn't Vivien see the danger she put them all in?

Faith and Cad walked up the steps of the Free French HQ in Carlton Gardens. Faith was looking forward to the meeting; Paul Daubert had sounded charming on the telephone the previous week. Cad, she knew, had different expectations. His views on the Gaullists were often unprintable.

Besides Cad seemed even more on edge than usual. There had of course been the usual news of agents caught and killed, but Faith knew something else was nagging at him. She had been surprised how upset he was after their visit to Colin in hospital. The young man had arrived back safely after a long and hazardous journey walking over the Pyrenees into Spain.

Colin's behaviour had been strange. Initially, he had seemed pleased that Liz had been sent out to replace him as leader. Then, all of a sudden, his mood altered totally; he burst into tears and declared himself a failure. Cad had looked grim as they left the hospital. Although fit physically, Colin was clearly a mental wreck.

'Goddammit! He's so young,' Cad had muttered angrily.

Faith thought she understood the tensions inside Cad. His son Julian was undergoing training at the moment and would soon be sent overseas. Cad's marriage was one of little substance; but Faith knew that, despite his protestations to the contrary, he adored his only child. At Colin's bedside, Cad had had a terrible premonition of his own son's future.

Paul Daubert greeted Faith and Cad with charm and courtesy. He was in his forties, a good-looking man who obviously enjoyed the good life but was no playboy. Faith knew that he was just the sort of person whom Cad found difficult to warm to – too much of the lounge lizard for his liking.

Paul Daubert shook Cad warmly by the hand.

'I am so glad to meet you,' he said. 'The General has spoken of you.'

‘I can imagine. We don’t always see eye to eye,’ Cad remarked dryly.

‘I am sure we can rectify that . . . with better liaison arrangements.’

‘Let’s hope so.’ Cad then introduced Faith. ‘My right hand, Faith Ashley.’

Faith liked the strong grip of the Frenchman’s handshake. ‘How do you do,’ she said, smiling up at him.

‘We have met before,’ Daubert mentioned.

‘Oh?’ She looked surprised, sure she would have remembered this man if she had met him before.

‘In Paris, I think. Weren’t you working at the British Embassy before the war?’

‘Yes.’

‘We met at some function there.’

Faith could see that Daubert’s charm was all part of his diplomatic background.

Cad had had enough of small talk. ‘I’ve another meeting later, so if we could get down to business?’ he said with an edge to his voice.

The business did not go very smoothly and Faith noticed how often the personalities of the two men gave rise to conflict. The main point of divergence was over centralization of the Resistance. The Outfit’s *sine qua non* was that no one should know what anyone else was doing.

Cad tried to find some way through the disagreements.

‘So we do accept the need for our organizations to work closely together to achieve a common aim.’

‘The liberation of France!’

‘It therefore follows that we should use the same *modus operandi*.’

‘I suppose from that that you wish us to change our ways?’

'Centralization is all very well, but in my view it's already caused a serious threat to security in France and—'

Paul leaned forward angrily. 'That is your view. I happen to think otherwise.'

'The Outfit has operated from the word go on the principle of fragmentation – small groups that only liaise with each other through HQ in London.'

'And are you telling me that hasn't led to problems?!'

'Of course it has, but . . .'

'I've worked in the field, remember?' said Paul. 'I've seen your people left high and dry. Wireless operator killed, no one knowing what the hell's going on.'

'I'd rather risk that than have every Tom, Dick and Harry knowing,' snapped Cad. 'At least they can't talk about what they don't know.' He sat back in his chair and drew deeply on his cigarette. 'We need each other. I am in charge here, but in the field we have to rely on you. Tomorrow, for example.'

'Ah yes,' Paul interrupted, slightly derisively. 'A big feather in your cap, you hope?'

'Vital to our cause, I think,' snarled Cad.

Faith tried to appease the two men. 'And vital to proving our effectiveness, Monsieur Daubert. Our authority needs the practical backing of the conventional forces – especially now, with plans for the invasion.'

Paul smiled at her.

'Of course I understand,' he said.

In a small attic, Emily listened intently to the messages which the BBC broadcast from London.

'Felicity would like the neighbours to get in touch. The cow jumped over the moon. Michael sends his love to

Susan. Aunt Doreen is taking the boys to lunch. All of Rodney's friends . . .'

Emily jumped up and switched off the wireless set; the important message had arrived. Hastily she pulled on a woollen sweater and a raincoat.

She hurried downstairs and was on her way out through the kitchen when Leon came in from his workshop. She bent down to kiss him in his wheelchair and he looked up at her anxiously.

'I must go now. Mustn't let them down,' she explained, trying not to show the tension which she felt.

Marie looked at the pair from the far corner of the kitchen, feeling a lump in her throat as these two reserved, undemonstrative people tried to take their leave of each other.

Leon looked at Emily with love and concern in his face.

'Whatever you're going to do . . . don't let us down. Come home safe.'

'I'll be back by morning. Don't worry.'

Emily gave Marie a tentative little wave and started towards the door to collect her bicycle.

'Good luck,' Marie whispered tearfully as Emily disappeared out of the house.

Leon spun his wheelchair across the kitchen and stopped next to Marie. 'It's like losing the others all over again,' he said softly.

Dressed as Victoire, Vivien cycled up to the radio station with her trailer full of fresh farm produce. Approaching the main gate where the guard was waiting to check people in and out, she showed her false identity card and was waved through. She parked her bike outside the side entrance to the main block and unloaded her basket of goods.

Jeanne was waiting for her and ushered her towards the supplies room. Vivien noticed that Jeanne seemed to be in a terrible state of nerves and jumped in terror when a guard crossed their path. But she pulled herself together and walked off up the corridor, with Vivien and the guard following. Vivien noticed the guard watching them closely as she unloaded the supplies she had brought.

As the women made their way to the laundry, the guard left them without a word. They began sorting through the washing and while they folded the linen, Vivien looked across at Jeanne. Something wasn't right . . . Vivien asked her if anything was the matter.

Jeanne avoided her gaze and muttered that she was OK. Half an hour passed in silence as they sorted out the bundles of laundry, then all of a sudden Jeanne stopped what she was doing and leaned across to Vivien.

'Go now,' she muttered urgently.

Vivien looked at her comrade in surprise.

'But it's early,' she whispered back.

Jeanne looked hard at her and hissed, *'Now!'*

Vivien didn't need to be told twice, but scuttled off quickly down the corridor towards the side entrance of the transmitting station.

Outside, darkness had fallen. Vivien crossed the compound from the main building to the outer wall, pausing for a moment to look back as she put her key in the side gate. Jeanne was deep in conversation, distracting the guard at the main entrance.

Vivien crept out of the station and gave the go-ahead signal with her torch before starting to make her way across the field towards the cover of the surrounding pine forests. Out of the corner of her eye, she caught sight of

Liz and Gordon lying in wait, ready to creep in and set the explosives.

Suddenly the silence of the night was shattered by Jeanne's voice: 'Run!' she shouted. 'It's a trap. Run for it!'

Machine-gun fire cut her down before she could say more. Vivien looked back for a second, then ran for all she was worth, darting in a zig-zag fashion across the field between the transmitting station and the woods.

'Get out of here!' she screamed, echoing Jeanne's last words. 'It's a trap!'

As Gordon and Liz started running with Vivien towards the trees, shots were fired at them from the compound. They had almost reached the relative safety of the woods when Gordon stumbled on a rabbit hole. He crashed to the ground and hauled himself up to follow the others, but as he stood up a shot found its target. Gordon fell, hit in the back; he tried to drag himself forward but slumped down again.

From the shelter of the woods, Emily saw what had happened. German soldiers were starting to emerge from the compound, firing as they ran towards the forest. Alsatian dogs were being released and were charging across the field. She took up a position a few trees distant from Josef.

'We'll cover you!' she cried.

Liz and Vivien heard her voice and ran back to help Gordon. As they did, Emily and Josef started firing out of the woods. By the time Liz and Vivien reached the Scotsman, he had struggled to his feet again, but he was badly injured and seemed unable to walk. The two women seized him under the arms and dragged him towards the forest.

As soon as they were under cover, Josef and Emily stopped firing and did their best to vanish into the trees.

They were out of ammunition and the first German soldiers were almost on them. Emily lost sight of Josef as she rushed towards the getaway van. She heard soldiers behind her, then realized it was only one man. He had evidently seen her; a shot whistled past and she could feel him gaining.

Suddenly she tripped on a tree root and fell heavily. She lay paralysed with fear as the soldier made his way towards her, too frightened even to scream as he aimed his gun at her head. She shut her eyes . . . nothing happened. She opened them to see the soldier fall to the ground, killed silently and expertly by Josef who had come up behind him with a knife.

Liz, Vivien and Gordon lay in the thick undergrowth of bracken, catching their breath. Gordon groaned softly.

'Are you all right? Gaspard?' Liz asked urgently.

Gordon didn't answer and Liz bent over him to look at his wound. He was bleeding heavily from both the front and back of his left shoulder. Vivien and Liz looked at each other anxiously as the sound of the Alsatian dogs became louder. There was nothing for it but to carry Gordon. They each draped one of his arms over their shoulders and dragged him through bracken and brambles which tore at their clothes and skin.

Gordon lapsed in and out of consciousness as they pulled him along. Eventually they reached a small river running through the forest and scrambled down the bank to the water. With any luck, the dogs would lose their scent here. Heaving Gordon across the stream and up the muddy bank, they staggered through the trees as far as a rutted forest track. Suddenly the dark figure of a man carrying a gun emerged from behind a tree. For a moment Liz's heart stopped, then she recognized the outline of Louis.

'Thank God!' she exclaimed. 'Please help us!'

Louis helped the women to lift Gordon into the back of the getaway van, then dashed round the front and climbed into the driver's cab. Just as he started up the engine, the sound of machine-gun fire could be heard from only yards away.

'Where's Zoe?' asked Vivien, as the van lurched off up the track.

'Where's Josef? Who knows?' Louis shrugged. 'We can't wait.'

CHAPTER 5

Dawn was breaking as the van pulled up at the back entrance to the Ferriers' shop. Liz and Vivien unloaded Gordon as quietly as possible and gave the signal to Louis that he should leave them. Then the women carried Gordon through the back-yard into Leon's workshop and laid the unconscious agent down on the bench.

Despite their best efforts, the noise had woken Marie. Wrapped up in her dressing-gown and wearing slippers, she came downstairs to find out what was going on.

Liz explained what had happened while Marie examined Gordon's wound. The bullet had gone straight through his shoulder; he had lost a lot of blood and his pulse was growing faint.

'He's still alive, but . . .' she said.

'We must get him to a hospital,' Vivien urged.

'They'll be searching everywhere. We wouldn't stand a chance,' Liz replied grimly.

Marie fetched wadding and disinfectant and was trying to dress Gordon's wound when Leon wheeled himself in from his bedroom alcove.

'What's happening?' he asked. 'Where's Zoe? She isn't with you?'

'The pulse is very weak,' said Marie. 'He may not last long.'

Again Vivien urged that he should be sent to hospital, but Liz shook her head.

'It's the first place they'll look.' She turned to Marie. 'Is there anyone who could help us: a doctor?'

Marie shook her head. 'They'll all be watched,' she said regretfully. Then a thought struck her. 'Unless Dr Fournier would come?'

Leon looked at his daughter.

'Michel? I don't know if we should involve him. He is very old.'

'I could go and ask.'

'You might lead the Germans straight here,' countered Liz.

They all stood looking at Gordon's body on the table. Suddenly, Leon spoke up.

'I will go,' he said. 'Who would suspect a useless old cripple? And we often play cards, Michel and I.'

Liz felt Gordon's pulse again. 'It's a risk,' she said. You can't go until the curfew lifts.'

'And Michel may refuse to come.' Evidently Leon did not wish to raise everybody's hopes. 'In the meantime, you can put him on my bed.'

'No,' said Liz. 'Upstairs will be safer.'

'In Zoe's room,' murmured Marie. 'What has happened to her?'

Liz only wished she knew.

Emily and Josef split up on the outskirts of town and she walked quickly through the streets, hoping to reach the Ferriers before too many people were up and about. She knew she must look a terrible sight – dirty and rumpled, with a large tear down the back of her jacket. She was just about to turn into the alleyway down the side of the shop when a voice made her start.

'Good morning, Zoe.' Emily turned reluctantly to speak to the woman.

'Oh, good morning, Annette,' she said politely.

Annette stepped forward and prodded her in the chest.

'Were you out all night, Zoe?'

'I missed the curfew. I was visiting a friend.' Emily cursed Annette's inquisitiveness.

'You must be careful of your family's reputation, my dear,' said Annette unctuously, studying the rip in Emily's coat. 'Was it a boy-friend?'

'I'd rather Aunt Marie didn't know about it,' said Emily. deciding that the best procedure would be to try to win Annette round to her side.

'They were up and about early this morning. I hope your boy's family put you up for the night,' Annette said knowingly.

They were interrupted by Marie. 'So there you are,' she said sternly to Emily.

'Good morning, Marie,' said Annette.

'Come in, Zoe. Your uncle and I both want to speak to you,' ordered Marie.

Emily walked shamefacedly into the shop, but as soon as the door was shut the two women fell on each other and embraced. Marie brought Emily up to date on what had happened and she immediately dashed up the stairs to see Gordon.

He lay on Emily's bed covered with blankets; he seemed to be drifting in and out of consciousness. Vivien and Liz sat on either side of him, Vivien wiping his face with a damp cloth. All Emily's instincts as a doctor's daughter came to the fore. Swiftly she called for more warm water and disinfectant and redressed Gordon's wound. She looked at him thoughtfully.

'At least he feels warm,' said Emily. 'The doctor's a long time coming.'

'He may never get here,' cautioned Liz. 'Leon might have been caught.'

'Oh, don't say that!' exclaimed Vivien.

Liz looked sharply at her. 'They must know a lot already, to have set that ambush.'

A hush fell on the room and all the women felt uncomfortable as Liz continued, 'There must be an informer.'

'Among the locals, you mean?' Vivien put in quickly.

'Josef saved my life,' Emily protested. 'And . . .'

Liz interjected, '*Somebody* betrayed us. We only got away because of Jeanne's warning.'

'Perhaps it was her,' suggested Vivien.

Liz stared at her, hardly believing what she had heard. 'It could have been any number of people. We can't trust anybody now.' She turned back to Vivien. 'You're the biggest security risk. You must go back to the château.'

'Wouldn't I be safer here in town?'

Liz shook her head. 'Wait for a bit, then go – and stay in hiding until you're contacted.'

She turned to Emily. 'You must leave as well.'

Emily looked puzzled. 'You mean to transmit?'

'No, not until things have quietened down. But you must move to a new safe house.'

Emily was upset. She had no desire to leave the Ferriers; they had become like second parents to her.

'What about Gaspard?' she asked.

'They will have to take care of him,' said Liz.

'But . . .'

'You're putting them in danger, too,' Liz explained.

'Perhaps the Germans already know all about us.' suggested Vivien.

'Perhaps,' agreed Liz quietly. 'We may be being watched and followed.'

Silence fell on the room yet again and the women looked at each other gravely. It was Vivien who finally spoke.

'We're in a hell of a mess, aren't we?' she said glumly.

Suddenly they heard someone climbing the stairs. A frail, elderly man poked his head round the door.

'You know,' he said querulously, 'I haven't practised for years?'

'Yes,' said Liz. 'Thank you so much for coming, Dr Fournier.'

Evidently shocked by the state of the British agent, he made a quick examination with shaking hands and asked how long he had been unconscious.

'Much of the time, these last few hours,' said Liz. 'Can you help?'

The doctor shook his head and looked serious.

'I'm sorry, but he hasn't got a chance.'

He saw the despair on Liz's face and added, 'Not without a hospital and proper facilities. He needs surgery, you see. This is a bad injury; internal bleeding.'

'We can't go to the hospital. Couldn't you operate?' Liz asked desperately.

The doctor looked at her over the top of his spectacles. 'My dear young lady, I was never a surgeon.'

'But if it's the only chance to save his life, you could try?'

'Please, I'll help,' Emily pleaded.

'This is delicate internal work,' explained the doctor. 'The muscle is badly torn and there may be chips of bone. You'll have to find someone else. I'm just an old man. My hands tremble . . . I forget things.' He hung his head, unable to cope with the desperation in the women's faces. 'I'm very sorry.'

'But you know what to do,' pressed Liz. 'So you could try.'

'You could save his life,' Emily asserted.

'I could kill him,' replied the doctor.

'He'll die if you don't operate – if you don't stop the bleeding,' Vivien put in.

The doctor stood still for a moment, gazing down at Gordon.

'I haven't the right instruments . . . and no anaesthetic. He might regain consciousness.'

Emily came forward with a suggestion.

'Marie knows the midwife down the road and she'll have some chloroform.'

Suddenly the doctor seemed to come to a decision.

'And we would need a great deal of hot water,' he said. 'And a much stronger light. The kitchen would be much better.'

'The walls are thin; it's too close to the shop. Could we wait until tonight?' Liz asked.

The old man shook his head again. 'Not unless you want a burial.'

He pulled a small brandy flask from his pocket and took a swig to steady his nerves.

Liz told Vivien to get back to the château before the doctor started operating on Gordon. Obediently Vivien crept downstairs, wondering whether or not to leave through the shop. Her mind was made up for her when she heard a woman's voice.

'So I said to Madame Durand,' the voice was saying, 'Zoe's a good girl. She wouldn't do anything to hurt her family.'

Vivien disappeared out of the back door.

Marie was getting increasingly irritated by Annette's presence in the shop. She pointedly squeezed past the other woman and started to rearrange the goods on some shelves. Then glancing into a mirror, she saw two German soldiers and jumped.

Her breathing returned to normal as she realized that the soldiers were simply peering in through the shop window at the goods on display. As the Germans walked off, her face relaxed.

'Something's troubling you.' Annette looked questioningly at the shopkeeper. 'Perhaps I can help?'

Marie looked at the older woman and wished for a moment that she could confide in a friend.

'Nothing's wrong,' she asserted. 'Did you want to buy something?'

'As if I could afford to!' sighed Annette.

It was only Marie's mention of Annette's youngest daughter, who had had to have a shotgun wedding, that finally moved the woman to leave the shop. A frisson of hostility passed between the two of them.

'I don't know what you're implying,' said Annette.

'Why, nothing. Excuse me, if I could just . . .'

Annette finally got the message.

'We've been neighbours for a long time,' she said stiffly. 'I was concerned for you, that's all.'

Marie watched her neighbour walk out of the shop with some misgivings. She hoped that Annette had not noticed the voices coming from upstairs.

Liz noticed with concern the number of small swigs that the old man took from his flask during the operation. Beads of sweat poured down his face as he tried to control his shaking hands. Emily was acting as his assistant. Liz's job was to hold the chloroform pad over Gordon's face and she tried not to look too anxious.

They all worked in silence. After what seemed like hours, the doctor straightened up and wiped his face.

'I'll do the stitching now,' he said to Emily, who handed him the needle and thread.

'Will he be all right?' she asked anxiously as the doctor swabbed the wound and started to insert the stitches.

'It was difficult to repair the muscle and the nerve. If he does recover, he may not have the full use of that arm again.'

'What are his chances of pulling through?' Liz asked.

'About even, I would say. Who will be looking after him?'

'I will,' Emily stated authoritatively.

Liz looked at the young girl and decided not to say anything immediately.

'You'll know in the next few hours whether or not he is likely to live,' said the doctor as he dressed the wound.

He told Emily to change the dressings regularly and check that the tissue looked healthy.

'Of course,' replied Emily. 'And thank you, doctor.'

'Don't thank me yet,' Dr Fournier said, as he began to clear up.

'We understand,' said Liz. 'But you tried and we're very grateful.'

'I worked through the last war. This was not so very different.' The doctor looked hard at the woman. 'If he does make a recovery, he'll need a long convalescence. Leon and Marie have suffered too much already; you must get this man away from here.'

Marie did her best to dissuade Emily from transmitting

to London that evening, but Emily would not be stopped. She had already missed one sked, and knew that everyone in Baker Street would be waiting for news. So she left Liz by Gordon's bedside, gave Marie a hug and slipped out at the back of the house.

Emily cycled hurriedly out of town and through the countryside. Approaching some trees, she dismounted and checked that no one could see her. Then she wheeled the bike to the edge of the copse and hid it in the undergrowth. She was just about to set off for the spot where she had hidden the radio when she heard the sound of approaching vehicles. Ducking out of sight, she watched as two German jeeps carrying soldiers passed by, looking on with mounting horror as they drove down the track which led to her destination.

As soon as the jeeps had disappeared out of sight, Emily came out of hiding and set off cautiously after them. The light was beginning to fade as she peered through the trees and tried to see what the Germans were up to. The jeeps were drawn up outside a woodcutter's hut and several of the soldiers were systematically going through the contents.

Emily crossed her fingers as she watched the search taking place. Then, what she dreaded most happened as one of the soldiers turned over a trough and something fell out of it with a thud. Bending down to investigate, he unwrapped a tarpaulin and discovered a battered leather attaché case. He took the case to his commanding officer, who opened it up and swore as he recognized the radio set.

Emily knew what would happen next. She tried to pick her way as quickly and quietly as possible through the trees, thankful at least for the evening gloom. As the shout went up from the German officer, ordering his men to search the wood, Emily started to run.

'Madame Rousset?'

'Oh, that'll be for me,' said Vivien, snatching the envelope from Juliette's hand.

'One of my cover names,' she added, as Juliette looked at her curiously.

Vivien walked out of the château, past the outbuildings where Emily – breaking all the rules – was finally making her transmission to London on her one remaining radio set. As Vivien walked through the stable yard, she looked up, saw the aerial hanging out of one of the hay-lofts, and frowned.

As prearranged, Emily went to meet her friend half an hour later in a secluded part of the château's grounds. Vivien was sitting on a wooden bench, soaking up some of the morning sun, and opened her eyes as Emily approached.

'Did you get through?' she asked.

'I was on for twenty minutes. Had to use the emergency frequency.'

'So the set was all right?'

'Yes, but I'll have to hide it somewhere else. It's the last one – I've asked them to send out two more.'

'They won't send anything until things have quietened down.'

Emily sat down next to Vivien.

'I had a letter this morning,' said Vivien, 'with Yvette's new address in Toulouse.'

'From her mother?' asked Emily, without thinking.

Vivien pulled a face.

'Sorry,' Emily apologized. 'I mean . . .'

'It's all right, Marguerite is her mother. I've been thinking about it all; why should Yvette give a damn about meeting me?'

Emily looked at Vivien with relief. 'So you've decided not to go to Toulouse again?'

'Of course I'm going!' cried Vivien.

'But . . .'

'I won't tell her who I am. After all, we may not get along; she might hate me.'

'The Germans have your description!'

'As Victoire, not me.'

'And what would Colette say if she found out?'

'That's why she mustn't. Be a pal, Emily.'

'When are you going?'

'Day after tomorrow.'

Emily looked at Vivien with suspicion.

'Is that why you let me transmit from here?'

'Oh, come on, Zoe! At least now they know back home what's happened.'

Cad had spent a testy last evening with his son, Julian, before he left on active service. Cad already knew that the Outfit's mission had backfired when the German station continued transmitting to the Atlantic U-boats. The next day, his humour was not improved by Emily's news.

He arranged a rendezvous with Paul Daubert on the outskirts of Epping forest. Daubert wasted no time in telling Cad that he considered the location quite ludicrous and each accused the other's side of incompetence. Matters became worse when Cad accused the French of betrayal. The two men stood in silence as storm clouds gathered overhead.

'Cooperation is the only way we're going to win this

bloody war,' declared Cad. 'Someone must have informed.'

In his eyes, the only possible informer was a French one.

'Possibly a British agent!' Daubert countered.

Cad glowered at the Frenchman, who continued, 'Has the arrest of my people never been caused by your half-trained adventurers trampling across my country?'

'That's hardly the issue now,' snorted Cad.

'You don't deny it.' Daubert pressed his point home. 'In the northern area? It was captured British who led to those arrests!'

'What matters now is that an assignment, which really counted, was turned into total disaster . . . and I'm left with a half-dead and useless explosives expert.'

The two men walked on, both fuming inwardly.

'We must try again,' said Cad. 'The new target is an engineering plant.'

'In Area 7 again?' asked Paul.

Cad nodded. 'They're making parts for enemy bombers.'

'The owner, will he cooperate?'

'I don't know. It's tricky and I'm leaving it up to our leader. The trouble is that none of our people have had specialist training.'

'You'll need help,' said Paul. 'Our leader in that area – Josef – is competent, I believe.'

Cad shook his head as they turned to walk back towards the cars.

'I don't think that will be good enough. I'll have to send somebody to back him up. It's obvious that we need a coordinator out there to overhaul security in all areas.'

'Or a joint working party?' Paul suggested wryly.

'The smaller the better. We need to rebuild. But first we

must find out what's going on; there have been too many unexplained arrests.'

As soon as Gordon was fully conscious, he started to worry about the danger in which he was putting Leon and Marie. Lying in bed, unable to do more than lift his head, he relived the night of the ambush over and over again.

'It was an ambush,' he said to Emily. 'But how did they know?'

'Don't think about it. We've got to get you better,' she told him.

Gordon tried to move his left arm, without success.

'Is this bit ever going to work again?' he asked despairingly.

'Course it will. *If* you don't move it now,' Emily insisted.

'Ever heard of a one-armed saboteur?' asked Gordon sourly.

Emily thrust a thermometer in his mouth to shut him up and went downstairs to fetch his lunch.

She had put a bowl of soup and a piece of bread on a tray and was about to go back upstairs when a voice made her almost drop the tray. She turned round to see Annette standing in the kitchen doorway.

'I didn't mean to startle you,' purred Annette. 'Having lunch upstairs, were you?'

'I sometimes take a meal to my room, when I'm not feeling too well.' Emily hoped that she sounded convincing.

'Staying out all night won't help you to recover from TB, you know,' Annette said.

'Are you looking for my aunt?' asked Emily brusquely. 'She's gone out looking for vegetables.'

'No, it's you I wanted to talk to, Zoe.' The older woman looked long and hard at the young girl. 'He is one of them, isn't he?'

Emily hoped her anxiety did not show.

'Well, he can't be a French boy!' said Annette, clarifying matters. 'Most of them are working in Germany now.'

Emily gave an inward sigh of relief as she realized what Annette was talking about. Suddenly the room exploded as Leon propelled his wheelchair into the kitchen.

'What are you doing in my kitchen, Annette?' he asked angrily. 'Please leave.'

Annette shouted back, equally incensed. 'There are things going on in this household that some of us demand to know about – like her staying out all night with a German!'

A terrible silence filled the room and then Leon roared, 'God in heaven, woman! Do you think I would allow my own niece to even speak to those monsters? After they shot me to bits in the last war? You stupid creature!'

Annette bristled with rage and then turned to Emily for confirmation or denial.

Emily acted for all her worth. 'Isn't it up to me who I go out with? I'm sorry, Uncle Leon, but there isn't much fun for a girl around here!'

Leon looked after her with astonishment as she rushed out of the kitchen.

Annette watched his reaction with shrewd eyes. Something about the exchange between Leon and Emily had not rung true.

The bus journey to Toulouse sped by, and Vivien tried to suppress her feelings of excitement. On arrival at the address she had been given, she thought she was going to experience another set-back, since at first the concierge appeared not to know Yvette's name. Then, with a look of distaste, she directed Vivien to the top floor of the large lodging house.

Dance music filtered down the stairwell from high above as Vivien walked up the ornate staircase. Once the house had been a large, stylish family home. Now it was divided up into shabby apartments.

The music came from the open door of an attic room. Vivien reached the top landing and paused for a moment to regain her breath. Then she summoned up her courage, walked towards the open door and looked in.

Immediately she recognized the girl dancing alone to the record as the girl in the photo. Yvette was pretty and vivacious. She was so absorbed in the rhythm of the music that she did not notice Vivien standing in the doorway until the record had come to an end.

'Are you looking for someone?' the girl asked.

'I was looking for you, Yvette,' said Vivien. 'May I. . . ?'

'Oh, come in.' Yvette gestured to Vivien to enter the room.

A complete contrast to the stuffy tidiness of the Moreaus, the room was colourful and chaotic, stuffed with posters and ornaments.

The pretty girl looked curiously at Vivien and asked whether she knew her.

Vivien introduced herself as Christine Rousset, a friend of the Moreaus. Immediately she had said that, she knew from the look on Yvette's face that she had picked the wrong white lie. A disagreeable scowl distorted Yvette's features and Vivien had to rectify the situation rapidly. She started to praise the girl's taste in decoration; this did the trick and Yvette began to relax.

Yvette made Vivien a cup of coffee and asked if she would excuse her while she changed. Vivien sat on the sofa, trying to take in everything. She sipped her coffee carefully; it was years since she had tasted real coffee and she wondered where Yvette had got it from.

After a short time, the girl emerged from behind a screen wearing a brightly coloured full-skirted frock. She twirled around in front of Vivien.

'What do you think, Christine?' she asked.

'It suits you very well.'

'Do you really think so? It's only borrowed.' Yvette performed a little pirouette. 'I wonder if my young man will like it?'

Vivien smiled as she caught Yvette admiring herself in the mirror. She was uncannily like herself at that age.

'Are you going out?'

'Yes – dancing, this afternoon.'

She came and sat down on the arm of the sofa as Vivien elaborated her cover story.

'Real coffee,' she murmured, enjoying the luxury. 'Have you managed to find a job, Yvette?'

The girl rose from the sofa and wandered round her room.

'All I want to be is an actress,' she sighed.

'And in the meantime?'

'Oh, I work in a bar.'

'Is that fun?'

There was a lull as Yvette stared hard at Vivien. 'I can't believe mother's worried about me. Have they sent you to spy?'

Vivien's laughter was so infectious that Yvette could not help but join in. As they wiped the tears of laughter from their cheeks, Vivien knew that she had broken through some kind of barrier between herself and the young woman.

'Tell me about your young man, Yvette.'

'Oh, he's really rather devoted. Quite sweet.'

'What's his name?'

'I think you *are* a spy!' Yvette laughed.

As she unbent towards her visitor, Yvette told how she had never felt herself part of the Moreau family.

'You know I'm not really her child – because she tells everyone that my mama abandoned me.'

Vivien felt desperately sad as Yvette tried to look defiantly uncaring.

'Don't look so shocked. But it's one reason I just couldn't wait to get away from home.'

'I felt that too at your age,' Vivien told her. 'I went on the stage before I married.'

'Really! Where? What did you do?'

'I was a dancer. I worked in Paris and on tour.'

'Oh, that must have been so exciting! Paris . . .'

'I had to give it up when I got married.'

'Because you married?' Yvette looked at Vivien with the self-confidence of youth and tossed her head in the air. '*I* shall never marry. I'll just have people love me to death, that's all!'

Both the women laughed at this outrageous declaration.

'You've got to tell me all about Paris,' urged Yvette. 'Mother disapproves madly of theatricals. Does she know about your lurid past?'

Vivien didn't reply immediately, then decided that she would have to risk telling the truth.

'Yvette, I have to tell you something – about myself, and you . . .'

Before Vivien could continue, there was a loud knock at the door and Yvette jumped up and ran across to open it. Her poise was reduced to nervous anxiety.

'There he is and I'm not ready;' she fretted.

'Jurgen!' she screamed with delight as she opened the door. 'You're on time as usual and I'm late as ever. Forgive me?'

'Hello, Yvie,'

Vivien could hardly believe her eyes as a young, clean-cut German lieutenant walked into Yvette's apartment and kissed her affectionately. Yvette took him by the hand and introduced him to her with a flourish, mischievously watching for Vivien's reaction.

'Lieutenant Jurgen Grunwald . . . Madame Rousset. She's a friend of mother's.' She laughed quickly. 'At least, she says she is.'

Vivien took hold of herself and quickly recovered from the initial surprise. She shook Jurgen by the hand and looked at him.

'Madame, I am intrigued.'

'Yvette is having a joke with both of us, I'm afraid. I'm a very dull friend of Madame Moreau.'

Jurgen sighed. 'Ah, Yvie has never spoken to me about her family.' He looked at Vivien curiously.

Vivien made small talk with Jurgen while Yvette finished getting ready for her date. The handsome blond youth filled her with deep unease and when Yvette tried to persuade Vivien to join them dancing, she pleaded transport difficulties, promising to come back and go out with Yvette another day. As Vivien shut the door to Yvette's room, she caught sight of the two young people in a passionate embrace. It was obvious that they were both very much in love.

*

Liz sat hidden behind some wine casks, waiting for Josef to arrive. She stiffened as she heard the sound of footsteps approaching slowly, making their way down the stone steps to the cellar. Peering round a cask, she saw Josef enter and look around with his sharp, beady eyes. She emerged from her hiding place and shook him by the hand.

'You're sure you weren't followed?' she asked anxiously.

Josef shook his head.

'What do you want that's so urgent?' he asked morosely.

Liz gestured at him to sit down next to her.

'The failure of the raid was a disaster for the organization and we need to know what happened. Your contact, Jeanne – could she have been an informer?'

'Of course not.' Josef sounded offended.

'Somebody told them, in time for the perfect ambush.'

'Jeanne shouted a warning; she saved lives and got killed for it.' Josef defended his colleague stoutly.

'But if it wasn't her?'

'We just don't know. Look, we just don't know.'

The Frenchman frowned and then came up with the possibility that was haunting Liz.

'It could be one of your lot, playing double or quits. Have you thought of that?'

She remained silent; the same idea had been haunting her. For the moment, she pushed it to the back of her mind and pushed on with more pressing arrangements.

'I've had instructions from London to get Gaspard away from here, as soon as he's fit to travel.'

'And?'

'We need your help.'

Josef gave a hollow laugh. The British were unbelievable at times.

'I thought you said his injuries were very bad.'

'They are. He'll never make it back to Britain. But things are quieter in Area 6 right now – we need to put him on to the escape line.'

'Any idea how we manage that?'

'I'm sure you can come up with something.'

Josef sucked on an evil-smelling cigarette and thought for a moment. Liz looked at the Frenchman and felt relieved; she could see that he would do his best to help.

Colin was sent out of London to a large Victorian convalescent house in the country. His recovery was painfully slow, and not helped by the fact that he regarded his pyschological problems as a sign of weakness.

Outside in the hospital grounds, Colin sat in the shelter of a high wall with a blanket tucked round him, watching a young patient try to walk on his new artificial legs. He felt almost envious of the young man learning to walk again. At least those injuries were physical.

'Enjoying the scenery?' a voice boomed out, making Colin start violently.

Kit placed his hand on Colin's shoulder. 'I'm sorry,' he said apologetically. He had had no idea that Colin was still in such a delicate state.

Colin smiled shakily at his old comrade as Kit sat down on the bench next to him.

'I don't get many visitors, now they've turned me out to grass here.'

'It's good to see you up and about. You're looking better.'

'I feel like a deserter. What am I doing here in hospital? Everyone else here is missing a limb.'

'If you were fit . . .'

'I know!'

'Give it time. You'll be back in the field all too soon.'

Colin turned to look at Kit. 'I'm surprised you're still in England,' he said.

Kit looked stony-faced, for Colin had touched a raw nerve.

'You know they sent Liz out,' he told Colin.

'To replace me? Yes, they told me.'

'I quarrelled with her, like a fool.'

'How did that happen?'

'I tried to stop her from going. Couldn't bear the thought of it, her being out there again.'

'She's doing a good job.'

'Yes, while I'm sitting around badgering Cad.'

Colin had his revenge by quoting back at him: 'If only you were fit?'

Kit smiled wanly. 'Liz is getting divorced.

'You've heard from her?'

'No, Faith told me . . . She'll be free before the year's out.'

'She means a lot to you, doesn't she?'

'We're not in touch. No messages . . . nothing. I can't stand this life, the bloody boredom – while she's at risk every minute.'

'They all are,' Colin said soberly.

A quietly-spoken and fastidiously dressed businessman in his late fifties, Raymond Sylvestre showed Liz round his engineering plant with great pride. She was dressed in a smart suit and carried a briefcase, very much in keeping with her cover job as an insurance representative. She noticed that all the workers were French, but that there was a considerable German military presence.

'It is very fine, my plant. Don't you think so?' Sylvestre asked. He was undoubtedly proud of his factory.

'It's most impressive, M'sieur,' acknowledged Liz.

'We had such a struggle to keep her ticking over. My best men are no longer here – but we have managed to keep going, nevertheless.'

'Except that you're no longer making parts for agricultural machinery.'

Sylvestre caught the acid tone in Liz's voice and hurriedly explained, 'The product is temporarily different. That is beyond my control.'

Liz looked across the rows of machinery churning out arms destined for German troops.

'You're manufacturing for the enemy, for their war against us. Don't you lie awake at night?'

Sylvestre looked at Liz pityingly.

'You don't understand. I built up this business from the earliest days. It was my first venture as a young man.'

'But look at it now.'

He gazed at Liz suspiciously. 'Why has Henri sent you?' he demanded.

'I wasn't sent by him,' whispered Liz. 'Is there somewhere we can talk in private?'

She followed Sylvestre up a metal staircase to his office overlooking the production floor. It was well soundproofed from the noise of the machinery working away down below. Sylvestre gestured at her to sit down opposite him at his desk.

'Who are you, Madame?' he asked coldly.

'I am personal assistant to Henri Lefèvre,' answered Liz, stating her cover as her eyes flitted round the room.

As Sylvestre began to justify his action, he wiped his forehead with a handkerchief.

'The Germans would have taken over my factory whether I remained in charge of it or not. And my workers – what would become of them if I abandoned the place?'

Liz sat upright in her chair and stared at the factory owner.

'How do they feel about their work – making parts for enemy bombers and tanks?' she asked.

Sylvestre looked at her with renewed suspicion.

'You speak like a foreigner. We have no choice! We've done all we can to slow production.'

'But you're still turning out the stuff!'

'That is unavoidable.'

'No!' Liz was insistent.

Sylvestre was brought up short by her abrupt remark and looked at her questioningly. 'Please explain yourself.'

Liz glanced out of the office window to make sure that there were no German soldiers close by before turning to Sylvestre once more.

'M'sieur Sylvestre,' she started, 'I can't tell you who I am, but I have received orders to destroy your plant.'

The Frenchman stared at her, not believing what he had just heard. 'Destroy it?' he gasped.

'To put it out of commission,' reiterated Liz. 'Yes.'

Sylvestre got up from his chair and went over to the window.

'Who gave these "orders"? By what authority?' he demanded.

'The highest authority, M'sieur.'

'Perhaps this is some kind of joke?'

'We're going to blow it apart . . . one way or another. I'm asking for your cooperation, in having . . .'

'No, my God! No!'

'You have no alternative.'

'I can refuse.'

'If you don't help us, M'sieur, we will bomb it – flatten the entire building. Some of your workers could be killed and your factory will never operate again. It's up to you.'

'This is blackmail,' he protested.

'Yes,' said Liz, 'it is.'

Gordon did not take kindly to the news that he was being sent to another area. It only confirmed his view that he was now totally useless to the Resistance. Emily did not tell Leon and Marie that it was her last night with them, but they soon guessed something was up when she insisted on cooking the evening meal.

She made a special effort. There were wild flowers in a vase to decorate the table, a checked tablecloth instead of the usual bare top, folded napkins and a special bottle of wine. She had cooked a version of Lancashire hotpot, but using rabbit instead of lamb.

Marie was intrigued by the strange dish and insisted that Emily give her the recipe. Emily herself had doubts about the meal and had little appetite. She was not quite sure whether it was something wrong with her cooking or the fact that she was dreading having to break the news of her departure.

Leon looked appreciatively at the label on the wine bottle.

'And where did you get this?' he asked her.

'A gift from a friend.'

'It isn't your birthday?' guessed Marie.

'No. I just wish I could thank you properly.'

'Whatever for?'

Leon and Marie looked at Emily as she struggled to articulate her feelings.

'You've been very good to me, both of you – and taking in Gaspard. And the other time when I was ill.'

Marie waved her hands dismissively as if to say 'don't be stupid.'

'Why are you saying all this, Zoe?'

Emily gazed at her plate intently. She couldn't bear to face Leon and Marie.

'I've been told to leave here,' she muttered. 'And I must. I'm sorry.'

Both of them were shocked by Emily's announcement and tried to persuade her to stay. On the verge of tears, she told them it was no good trying to persuade her.

'I hope I'll see you both again,' she gulped. 'Perhaps after the war is over?'

Marie was almost on the verge of tears herself.

'But even if you must live somewhere else, surely you could still visit us?' she asserted.

Emily shook her head sadly.

'I don't know if it will be possible. I've got to change my cover story.' She looked thoughtful as she remembered. 'There is one thing. My radio – the last one I've got. It's broken: the resistor, I think. I've tried, but I just can't fix . . .'

Marie looked appalled. 'You can't go from here and have no communications,' she insisted.

'That settles it.' Leon took command of the situation. 'You bring the radio to me tomorrow and I'll mend it if I can. Then you leave, if you really must.'

Emily looked at the two kind people who had given her more attention than her parents ever had.

'Thank you. I suppose it can't make any difference, just one more night.'

The Sylvestre that Liz met the following morning looked a changed man, haggard and considerably less dapper. Liz walked briskly into his office and closed the door behind her, sitting down opposite him without waiting to be asked.

'Good morning,' she said. 'So you've slept on it?'

She couldn't resist the little jibe at the expense of the collaborator.

Sylvestre snorted. 'Slept? That is not the word!'

'And?' Liz asked.

The Frenchman took a folded paper from the drawer in his desk and slowly opened it out. Smoothing the folds, he laid the paper on the desk; it showed a map and plans of the factory.

'My factory and works,' he explained.

'You agree to help us?' Liz was surprised by the change in attitude since the previous day.

Sylvestre nodded. 'If you agree to do as little damage as possible to my plant.'

Liz looked at the man and smiled at him.

'Thank you. It's better this way, you'll see.'

Sylvestre looked sadly at the plans.

'I know a little about explosives,' he volunteered.

'Someone will be sent to manage this job. We don't yet know who or when.'

Back in London, Cad gave Kit the news for which he had been waiting so long: he was finally to be sent back into action. Unlike some of his briefings, which were held in the bathroom of Parkgrove Mansions, he met Kit in the relative luxury of the old library.

Kit guessed that he was probably to be sent back when he received Cad's summons, but even so he could scarcely suppress his pleasure at the news. He wanted to know every detail about the job and Cad smiled at the man, thinking it was good to see Kit back on form again.

'You'll be working with the Gaullists, coordinating Resistance groups,' Cad explained.

'Across the country?' asked Kit, wondering whether he would be able to see Liz.

'Moving around constantly. We'll get you a good cover. There have been a lot of security lapses – possible betrayals.'

'I'll see to it. Thanks Cad.'

'You'll have your work cut out, getting them into shape as fast as possible.'

'When can I go?'

'There's one other job I want you for first. You're the only expert in explosives I've got available at present and we need you for an assignment in Area 7.'

There was a pause as Kit took in what Cad had just said.

'Seven? I'll do it,' he said rapidly, realizing that he would be with Liz again.

Cad studied Kit carefully.

'I've been uncertain as to whether to ask you to go there, but we're desperate.'

'Why ever not, for God's sake?'

'I think we both know why,' said Cad. 'Elizabeth's leading that circuit.'

'And so?'

'And you know, of course, that any attachment between agents in the field is too dangerous to contemplate.'

'Can't you trust my judgment?'

'I only mentioned this for your sake, Kit. Glad I can rely on you.' He slapped Kit on the shoulder. 'Incidentally, our last sabotage man in that circuit was shot.'

Dusk was falling as Emily helped Gordon downstairs. He was still terribly weak and unsteady on his feet and his left arm dangled uselessly by his side. Marie gave him a bowl of coffee as he sat by the stove, waiting for Liz to arrive.

Liz walked down the street towards the Ferriers. She was so concerned to make sure that no one was following her that she failed to notice a curtain twitch as she passed Annette's house. Going round to the back of the shop, she knocked very softly on the door and Marie ushered her in. Through the gloom, Liz could see Gordon being helped on with his coat by Emily.

'What are you doing, still here?' Liz asked severely.

'I'm leaving tomorrow, Colette.'

'Make certain of that!' Liz snapped and went across the room to Gordon.

Leon embraced Gordon and shook his right hand.

'It's time to go,' Liz announced as the two men drew back from each other.

Emily gave Gordon two kisses on each cheek and wished him the best of luck. Emily, Leon and Marie all stood in silence for some time after Liz had disappeared out of the back door with Gordon leaning on her.

It was with painful slowness that Liz and Gordon made their way up the road past the Ferriers'. Hobbling through the dark streets, they had to hide in the shadows a couple of times as a German patrol passed.

After what seemed to Liz an eternity, they reached

their destination – a small undertaker's shop. Liz knocked on the shop door with the prearranged signal and they were admitted by a small birdlike man. He had a coffin waiting for Gordon to climb into.

At the Ferriers, Marie had gone back to bed but Leon and Emily were huddled over her radio set in his workshop.

'So that's what was wrong,' said Leon, putting the set back together.

Outside there was the sound of a lorry braking, followed by shouting. Leon and Emily looked at each other with the fearful realization that they were about to be raided. Emily leapt to her feet and started towards the back door, but Leon whispered that she was too late – the shop would be surrounded.

The sound of soldiers trying to break down the front door echoed through the building, and Leon gestured to Emily to hide under his bed. Half a dozen SD men in their grey uniforms stormed through the house. Two ran upstairs, knocking Marie out of their way as she came down in her dressing gown.

Emily watched in terror from beneath the bed as two other soldiers searched through Leon's workshop. They had obviously been tipped off. They threw all his work on the floor. Leon positioned his wheelchair across the entrance to his sleeping alcove, to try and protect Emily.

A howl of triumph went up as the radio set was found. The man spun round on his heels and turned threateningly to Leon.

'Do you think I would ever tell you?' shouted Leon as the man came towards him. He bent down and picked up a clock that had been thrown on the floor and lobbed it towards the approaching SD. Two more men came into the workshop and they all set on Leon.

While Leon struggled with his attackers, Emily seized the opportunity to crawl out of the workshop. Leon saw her go out of the corner of his eye and prolonged his fight as long as he could, to give her time to escape.

Once outside in the backyard, Emily started to run. As she pounded down the dark streets, a funeral car containing a coffin passed her by. She was just about to round the corner into the main square when she was stopped in her tracks by the sound of a single gunshot.

CHAPTER 6

Emily turned and made her way back to the shop inching her way down the street, hiding in the shadow of the overhanging houses. From a safe distance, she watched the activity outside the Ferriers' shop. Her worst fears were confirmed when she saw two SD men carry out a body. Unceremoniously, they flung it on the back of their lorry, as if it were a sack of coal. There was no doubt that Leon was dead.

As an old, cowed woman was escorted out of the shop and into a waiting car, it took a couple of seconds for Emily to recognize Marie. With a horrible sense of despair, she felt that she might never see her again.

As the German convoy drove off, leaving the street to return to silence, Emily leaned back against the brick wall. Tears rolled down her cheeks, and she took a couple of deep breaths to steady her emotions. A sense of guilt overwhelmed her; she was responsible for Leon's death and Marie's capture. If only she had left when Liz had told her to go, none of this would have happened.

The next morning, Vivien made her way through the outbuildings of the château. She checked that no one was around, then went into the stable to use the dead-letter drop. She had removed the brick from the wall and was about to put the message into the empty cavity when a noise behind her made her freeze. Slowly, fearing the worst, she turned round.

There was Emily, tired and dishevelled, emerging from behind a bale of hay.

'Christ, Zoe!' exclaimed Vivien. 'You gave me a fright!'

Emily swallowed hard and summoned up all her resources to speak, but nothing came out. She just gazed up at Vivien like a Dickensian urchin. Vivien thought she had never seen such a pathetic, frightened sight.

'Are you all right?' Vivien asked, although it was patently obvious that Emily was far from all right.

'They've . . . shot Leon and arrested Marie.'

Before Emily could explain any more, she crumpled up. Tears poured down her cheeks and she sobbed uncontrollably. Vivien rushed over to Emily and put her arms round the young girl.

As soon as Juliette had gone out for the morning, Vivien smuggled Emily into the château, so that she could have a bath and something to eat. She forced Emily to eat a couple of boiled eggs and Emily couldn't help reflecting that, despite her flashy exterior, Vivien would have made a good mother.

Later that day, in a small side chapel of the church at Arbon, Emily lit a candle to the madonna and knelt down to pray. Perhaps God could absolve her guilt. She was miles away when a voice whispered.

'How much does she know?'

Emily roused herself and looked sideways at the woman praying next to her. It was Liz.

'Marie Ferrier? How much does she know?' Liz muttered out of the corner of her mouth.

'I . . . I'm not sure,' stuttered Emily.

Liz was impatient. 'You must have *some* idea.'

Emily gulped hard.

'Well, she's met you and Solange, of course.'

'But does she know names and addresses?'

'No, I wouldn't think so.' There was a pause before Emily continued, 'I'm not sure.'

Liz was quietly relieved.

'That's something, I suppose – Not that it will help Marie.'

Emily tried to stop herself crying.

'I'm sorry, Colette. I should have moved when you said.'

'What's done is done,' replied Liz brusquely. 'The main thing now is to find you a new safe house and a fresh cover.'

'Yes. Do you know where they've taken her?'

'Marie? No. But the SD will want to question her, that's certain.'

'Oh God,' moaned Emily, knowing that 'questioning' was only a euphemism for torture.

After a pause, Liz asked Emily how it had happened.

'Somebody must have talked – they knew what they were looking for.'

Liz pursed her lips, pondering what course of action she should take next. This time it was Emily who broke the silence.

'What are we going to do with no wireless?'

'I thought you'd asked for two more to be sent out.'

'I did, but it'll take weeks unless we tell them how urgent it is. And how do we do that?'

'I don't know.' Liz thought for a moment and then said, 'I'll have to try and get a message through Area 6.'

'Do you know anyone?'

'Not really. But when I was working with Faith back in London, she told me of a café in Mont-de-Marsan where some of the circuit meet.'

The women resumed their praying as a priest swept past them and into the vestry. As soon as he was out of the way, Liz turned to Emily.

'You'd better go. And, Zoe,' Liz spoke kindly, 'you must try to forget about Marie. Lie low for the time being and keep on the move. That's an order.'

She placed on the altar rail a small slip of paper which Emily picked up.

'Here, go to this address and ask for Madame Burnet. Just say you're Zoe and she'll help you. OK?'

Emily nodded and put the piece of paper in her pocket. As she rose to her feet, she quickly made the sign of the cross and bowed to the statue of the Virgin Mary. Liz remained apparently deep in prayer as Emily walked out of the church.

Emily made her way to Montaud. The address which Liz had given her was in the poorest part of the town, not far from the station. The streets were narrow, more like alleys, with washing draped across like bunting between tall tenement buildings.

Double-checking that she was not being followed, Emily went up to her new safe house. She made her way through a half-open door to a scruffy courtyard where a large overweight, over-made-up woman sat on a chair in the sun, stroking the cat on her lap.

'Yes, my dear?' asked the woman, without removing the cigarette from the side of her mouth.

'I'm looking for Madame Brunet . . .'

The woman put the cat down on the ground and eased herself up out of her chair, holding her hand out to Emily.

'That's me,' she said with a voice that spoke of too much drink and too many cigarettes. 'What can I do for you?'

'I'm Zoe,' Emily whispered.

The woman stared, in obvious amazement that this young girl could possibly be a secret agent. Emily felt scared when a tarty young girl and a middle-aged man came through the courtyard and went upstairs into the house. As soon as they had disappeared, Madame Brunet led Emily towards the building.

'You'd better come with me, dear,' she said kindly.

Emily was confused by the amount of activity which seemed to be going on in the house. A young man passed her on the stairs, hurriedly slipping on his jacket; a young girl dressed only in a slip wandered down a corridor.

When they reached the top of the house, Madame Brunet threw open a door and ushered Emily in. It was a small, bare room with an iron bedstead and not much else.

'All right?' whispered Madame Brunet.

'Oh yes,' answered Emily, relieved at having a bed of any kind.

As the woman turned to leave, she gave Emily a knowing look and warned her to lock the door. It was not until she had followed these instructions and flung herself on to the bed that she realized what sort of house she was staying in. The sounds of coarse laughter, slamming doors and sexual activity washed over her. Emily wept herself to sleep.

Back in her safe house, Liz made preparations for her trip to Area 6. It was totally against regulations to cross from one area to another, but she could think of no alternative solution to their problems.

She sat at her table and wrote a coded message asking for new radio sets. Then she rolled up the small piece of paper as tightly as possible and carefully hid it inside a cigarette from which she had removed the tobacco. She replaced the cigarette in the corner of a half-empty packet, which she put back in her handbag.

Checking briefly in the mirror on her wall that she looked presentable, she put on some lipstick, pulled her hat into place and set off.

At Mont-de-Marsan, Liz had no problem in finding the café, which took up almost one side of the main square. It was a large place full of mahogany and mirrors. An awning was stretched out across the pavement, on which were set a number of tables and chairs.

Liz paused at the entrance to the café and looked round surveying the place. She pretended to look for someone, and chose a table in the corner where she could watch people enter the café.

She managed to make an anis last for well over an hour and was just beginning to wonder what to do next when a young man walked through the café doors. He was tall, bespectacled and wearing a blue boiler-suit. Pulling out a newspaper from his back pocket, he sat down at the next table to hers.

Liz took her packet of cigarettes out of her handbag and removed one, then turned to the young man and asked for a light. He rummaged in his pocket, brought out a box of matches and lit one as she leaned towards him with a cigarette in her mouth.

'I know this is breaking the rules,' Liz whispered, 'But I recognize you from our training course at the Manor.'

The young man started in surprise, but instantly regained his poise as he proceeded to light Liz's cigarette.

'Colette,' she said, introducing herself. 'Area 7. I'm in

a bit of trouble and I need to get a message through to London urgently.'

Raising her voice, she offered him a cigarette. He looked at her knowingly and took the one that she had half pulled out of the packet. This he put in his mouth and was just about to light it when Liz told him not to do so.

He coolly blew out the match and popped the cigarette behind his ear. Liz scanned the room nervously in case they had been watched. Fortunately, no one seemed interested in them. She downed the last of her drink and bade the young man farewell.

All the extra searches and intensified military activity in the area did not deter Vivien from her plan to re-visit Yvette. Yvette greeted her warmly and gave her another welcome bowl of real coffee. Vivien listened in dismay as the girl gabbled on; she seemed to have a totally shallow and opportunistic outlook on life. A new pair of shoes was more important to her than the fact that she was fraternizing with the enemy.

Part of Vivien sympathized with Yvette's longing for some glamour in a rather drab life, but there was no getting away from the fact that her daughter was a collaborator.

'Does he love you?' Vivien asked the girl.

Yvette pouted and looked knowing. 'In his own way,' she giggled.

'And you?'

Yvette laughed. 'Oh, Christine! You sound just like my mother!'

For a second Vivien was disconcerted, then she joined in with Yvette's laughter.

'I'm sorry,' she apologized. 'I'll shut my big mouth. Tell you what, I'll treat you to lunch!'

This would be an opportunity to spend some of the vast amount of French francs with which she had been issued in England, she thought.

'How about your hotel?' she suggested. 'I'd like to see where you work.'

The hotel where Yvette worked behind the bar was a large place in the grand style. An ornate double staircase swept down into the panelled and mirrored foyer. Tables and chairs filled the foyer and to one side was the mahogany bar.

As the two women walked through the foyer to the dining room, Vivien noticed to her dismay that most of the clientele were German officers. They ordered a light lunch, which Yvette ate with gusto, but Vivien toyed with her meal even though food was in short supply at the château. Under other circumstances she would have enjoyed herself; the good food, the crisp linen tablecloths and attentive service would have brought out her sybaritic side. As it was, the heavy German presence put her on edge.

When Yvette had finished eating, she sat back and asked Vivien whether Marguerite ever talked about her.

'Who?' asked Vivien, without stopping to think. Her mind was miles away, wondering how Emily was managing.

Yvette gave her new friend a funny look, then explained, 'My foster mother, of course!'

'Oh well, yes, of course,' said Vivien. 'She seemed very proud of you.'

Yvette looked at her with disbelief. 'Proud of me. That's a joke!'

'Why?' Vivien immediately recalled the disapproving way in which Marguerite had spoken about the girl.

'She was proud of Madeleine all right,' Yvette said bitterly, 'but I was just another mouth to feed.'

'I think you're being rather hard on Marguerite,' said Vivien, trying to stand up for Madame Moreau. 'After all, she didn't have to adopt you.'

Yvette shrugged her pretty shoulders. 'My mother didn't *have* to abandon me . . . but she did.'

Vivien fell silent and wondered whether to tell her the truth. She was just about to embark on her story when the girl jumped up from the table, clapping her hands with pleasure.

'Jurgen!' she shouted.'

The young man stood at the entrance to the dining room. Seeing Yvette, he smiled with pleasure and walked over to their table. He kissed Yvette passionately on the lips and greeted Vivien amiably as he sat down at their table.

'Well, my young friend, you're doing rather well!'

Jurgen jumped to his feet and the two women looked up to see an officer in the SD.

'Enjoying the company of *two* charming ladies.' he laughed unpleasantly.

Jurgen joined in the laughter and introduced the man.

'This is an old friend of my father's, Sturmbahnführer Voller.'

'May I join you, Mademoiselle?' Voller asked and sat down rather too close to Vivien for her liking, looking at her with a wolfish grin.

Maintaining her composure with difficulty, Vivien tried to be coolly charming to him. All her acting skills were once again called upon. As she spoke to Voller, she failed to notice a thin Frenchman in a business suit watching their table with interest. Soon afterwards, he folded up his newspaper and left the dining room.

Back in London, everyone was frantic with worry about what had happened to the circuit. Emily had now missed two skeds and although that didn't necessarily mean trouble, Cad was very jumpy. Relations with the Free French were still touchy, and he didn't want another disaster so soon after the foul-up at the transmitting station.

The germs of a suspicion that the circuit might have been infiltrated prompted Cad to pay Colin a visit at the convalescent hospital. Colin's morale was considerably improved and he no longer seemed so self-obsessed, even advising Cad on what to buy Julian for his 21st birthday. Cad was pleased to hear that Colin might be discharged soon, but the young man had no recollection of anything that could help.

Cad returned to his office to find two pieces of news. The first was Liz's message, which had arrived via Area 6. The second was in the form of an official telegram.

'Well?' asked Faith, coming into his office. 'Good news?'

Cad shook his head numbly and handed her the telegram. Faith read that Cad's son, Julian, had been killed in action only two days before his 21st birthday.

One day, when she was dozing on her bed in the brothel, Emily was woken by a familiar sound: the noise of screeching brakes. She leapt from her bed and peered out of the grimy window.

Madame Brunet's establishment overlooked the railway

lines and Emily saw two trucks in the yard by the railway siding. German soldiers jumped out and started ordering civilians out of the backs of the vehicles. Emily scanned the people waiting for deportation, desperately hoping to see Marie, but she was too far away to be able to make out anyone's face. She grabbed her jacket from the back of the door and dashed off downstairs and out of the brothel.

Emily had to force herself not to run to the railway yard, knowing she must do nothing to draw any attention on herself. In the yard, a small crowd of people had gathered to watch the deportees being herded into groups. Emily pushed her way to the front of the crowd and stared hard at the prisoners. Suddenly, she drew in her breath sharply.

Marie was scarcely recognizable. Her face was cut and swollen; one eye was almost closed. For a second, the two women's eyes met and Marie smiled sadly and gave her a slow shake of the head. Before Emily could give any indication that she had seen her, Marie was manhandled on to a cattle truck.

Sadly Emily returned to her room. At least Marie was alive, but for how much longer? She knew that those cattle trucks would be destined for a concentration camp, either in the north of France or in Germany itself.

Fortunately, Emily had little chance to brood. Liz wanted her back in the field, and she would have to adjust quickly to her new identity as Nathalie Maupert, a chambermaid in the nearby town of Arbon.

Her new papers were good forgeries, bearing the photograph she had brought from England, with the correct stamps. She had to dye her hair with henna to fit the description of redhead on the ID, and become used to wearing some very unflattering wire-framed round glasses.

Liz was worried by the lack of news from London. Each trip she made into Area 6 made her feel increasingly vulnerable. Finally, after several fruitless visits, the message came through:

'WILL SEND THREE NEW PIANOS STOP ALSO NEW SABOTAGE INSTRUCTOR VICTOR STOP PLEASE ARRANGE DROP STOP.'

It was the P.S. which made her smile: BLOODY GOOD TO KNOW YOU'RE STILL THERE STOP. She could almost hear Cad saying that.

A week later, Liz watched the huge full moon with apprehension as she heard the sound of an approaching Halifax bomber. Then, out of the darkness, the plane circled overhead and a solitary parachutist descended, outlined against the black night sky. Liz peered at the tall figure striding towards her, carrying his parachute. She and Josef went forward to greet him as he raised his hand in greeting.

'Good evening,' whispered a familiar voice.

Liz gasped as the moonlight caught the side of Kit's face.

'Kit!' she exclaimed, without thinking.

'Victor now!' he admonished her.

She stood still, completely at a loss for words. What the bloody hell was Cad playing at, sending Kit out to join her circuit?

'Well, don't I even get a hello?' he asked.

Despite herself, Liz broke into a broad smile and flung her arms around him.

'God, I've missed you!' Kit whispered in her ear.

Liz's emotions were more complex. She was beginning to get the circuit back on its feet, not to mention getting her own feelings under control, and now Cad had sent out the one person who could be relied upon to throw her into confusion.

As soon as all the cannisters had been collected, the team disappeared into the night and Kit returned with Liz to her safe house. As they sat opposite each other in her flat, Kit tried to explain why he had been sent out.

'There was no way André could make it back, so Cad decided to send me instead.'

Liz mulled over Kit's news, then went over it again with him. 'So you'll work with us on the factory job and then start coordinating all the other resistance groups?'

'That's about it, yes.' Kit grinned at Liz over the bottle of red wine she had opened. 'It'll be quite like old times.'

Liz ignored his remark and ploughed on with the essentials.

'I'll need to know your cover story,' she told him.

Kit handed her his papers as he gave her a run-down of his new persona.

'I'm Victor Bichelot, salesman in agricultural spare parts. A step up from peasant farmer, I suppose.'

Liz gave no sign of understanding his reference to the time when they had worked together in Area 3. She simply studied his papers gravely and handed them back to him.

'You ought to know I've established new security arrangements for liaising with each other . . .'

Kit gazed at her sadly. 'You're still angry with me, aren't you, Liz?'

Liz avoided his look.

'Of course I'm not. And Kit, out here I'm Colette, remember? You're Victor. Let's stick to the rules. OK?'

Kit was thrown slightly by Liz's determination to keep her distance from him, but covered his discomfiture with a tight smile.

'OK. You're the boss,' he said.

However the next day Liz wondered how true that statement was. She had a worrying meeting with Josef, when she outlined Kit's involvement in the scheme to blow up the factory. Josef was uncharacteristically dismissive of the venture and expressed the hope that Kit would turn out to be more competent than André.

It was not Josef's scepticism which perturbed Liz – she sensed that he was holding something back from her. This impression only increased as he made up reasons to delay the scheme. It was only after some persistent prodding that Josef revealed his worries to Liz.

One of his couriers had been in Toulouse the previous week and had spotted Vivien lunching at the same table as the local SD chief, Voller. Liz looked at Josef in horror. All her worst suspicions about Vivien seemed to be confirmed.

Emily was trying on her new spectacles and looking at herself in a small hand mirror when she heard a commotion coming from the street. Madame Brunet burst into the room to tell her that soldiers were searching the whole area and that she must leave.

Carrying only a small bag containing the minimum of possessions, Emily was smuggled out of the bordello by the back stairs.

Noticing a bicycle propped up outside someone's house, she looked round to make sure the coast was clear before taking the machine and making off for the countryside. A couple of miles outside town, Emily dismounted. Taking cover behind the tombstones in a cemetary, she ate an apple which she had saved for her lunch.

It was as she tossed the apple core away into the undergrowth that the sound of a twig snapping alerted her to the presence of other people. Two figures with guns rose up from behind a couple of tombstones; they wore black berets and leather jackets, like the Milice. Emily froze with fear and slowly got to her feet, holding her hands above her head.

As the two men approached her, she noticed with relief that they were not police but young men in the Maquis. After some initial suspicion on both sides, Emily explained who she was and asked if the young men knew of Luc, Marie's son. They nodded to each other and volunteered to take her to their hideout.

The Maquis hide-away was an isolated, half-ruined farmhouse situated on a slight hill so that it commanded a view of all the surrounding countryside. The farm was built in the shape of a hollow square and in the centre was a cobbled courtyard littered with men and munitions. In one corner a bonfire blazed, providing heat for the men and for cooking.

A meal was in progress when Emily arrived. Immediately, she was introduced to the assembly. One of the older men who was acting as cook motioned her to sit at the makeshift table and gave her a bowl of soup, which she accepted gratefully.

She gave her undivided attention to the soup, very conscious that all the young men were staring at her in fascination. As a shadow fell across the table, she looked up into the face of a serious young man who bore a close resemblance to Marie.

'You asked about Luc Ferrier?' he said.

Emily hesitated for a moment, then stood up and shook him by the hand. 'Hello, Luc. I'm Zoe.'

She hurriedly finished her soup and walked with Luc up into the woods behind the ruined farmhouse. There they sat next to each other on a large log while she told him what had happened to his mother and grandfather as simply as possible.

For a few moments the young man sat in silence, then he jumped to his feet and yelled out. 'Bastards! Bloody murdering bastards!'

Averting his face from Emily, he kicked the pine cones. Then he brushed his face with his arm and turned back to her.

'How did she look? My mother? When you saw her at the station?'

'Calm. She was a very brave woman, Luc.'

He stared at Emily questioningly. 'Had they tortured her?'

Emily paused for a moment and then lied.

'I don't know; it didn't look like it. She could have told them nothing of any use anyway – they must have known that.'

Luc came and sat down next to her again.

'So how did *you* manage to escape?' he asked angrily.

Emily had been dreading that question.

'Your grandfather helped me. Without your mother and him, I would have been caught too. They saved my life.'

'You must be important,' Luc growled.

Emily said nothing. She looked away as tears welled up in her eyes.

'I'm sorry,' Luc murmured. 'I didn't mean to . . .'

'No.' Emily couldn't blame the lad for his outburst. 'I understand how you feel . . .'

The two of them sat in silence until the sun started to go down, then Emily stood up and turned to Luc.

'Well, I'd better be on my way,' she announced.

Luc urged her to come and stay at the ruined farmhouse, but Emily refused politely. She had no wish to bring disaster on the sole survivor of the Ferrier family. They shook hands and Luc watched from the woods as Emily made her way down to the road in the distance. Then, to his surprise, he saw her stop in her tracks and walk back towards him.

Kit's visit to Sylvestre's factory proved to be more interesting than he had anticipated, when he was shown round in his guise as agricultural representative. In fact, the noise from the machinery was so great that the men could talk without fear of being overheard.

'Your best bet,' advised Sylvestre as they walked past a row of machines making precision parts, 'is to go for the mounting blocks on these machine tools.'

'How easily can they be replaced?' asked Kit.

'They have to come from Germany. Four weeks minimum – and that's just getting them here.'

Sylvestre had to leave Kit on the factory floor while he went up to his office to take a telephone call and Kit carried on his inspection alone. Walking to the end of the large workshop where it was much quieter, he became aware of a deep humming sound coming from behind a large steel door. A notice on the door in French and German forbade anyone to enter.

Glancing around to check that no one was watching him, Kit cautiously tried the door handle. It opened easily. He darted into the forbidden room and shut the door behind him, staring in amazement at a huge transformer throbbing and humming. To one side was a control panel with an empty seat in front of it. An opened newspaper and a half-smoked cigarette in an ashtray, however, suggested that there was someone about.

Kit looked round carefully and was inspecting the control panel when the door suddenly opened and a man wearing overalls but with a gun in his belt walked in.

'Who the hell are you?' the guard demanded.

'Monsieur Artaud,' Kit introduced himself coolly. 'I'm an associate of Monsieur Sylvestre.'

The guard jabbed a finger at the door. 'Can't you read? This is strictly off limits.'

'I'm on an official inspection from the Chartoire plant. Didn't they tell you?'

'Chartoire?' The guard lost some of his antagonism. 'First I've heard of it. I must ask you to show me your papers.'

Kit stood where he was. 'I assure you, you have only to call up Monsieur Sylvestre.'

'That's as may be,' said the guard gruffly.

Kit was just about to produce his ID documents when Sylvestre walked in; he nodded at the guard and hustled Kit out of the room. Sylvestre reproached Kit for his carelessness, but when pressed as to what the forbidden room contained, the Frenchman seemed very evasive. He passed it off as unimportant, only an auxiliary generator, but Kit was not convinced.

Liz and Vivien met in the park at Montaud.

'Have you seen Emily recently?' Liz asked.

'Not in the last few days, no, but that's not unusual. We liaise through the dead-letter drop. I thought that was the rule.'

Liz nodded her head.

'It is.'

Liz sounded out Vivien about her knowledge of Toulouse.

'You don't have any friends there?' she asked.

Vivien shook her head, then asked why Liz wanted to know.

'It's just that we may have to widen the circuit to include Toulouse in the lead-up to liberation,' Liz lied. 'Any local knowledge will obviously come in useful.'

'It's changed a lot since I was last there,' Vivien replied, 'but I'm game to try.'

'Good. I'll let you know when.'

Liz stood up to go and leaned over the pram. Under the pretext of admiring the baby, she tucked a small manilla envelope under the blanket; it contained the messages for Zoe's next sked.

Both women were left uneasy by the exchange. Vivien felt sure that Liz knew more than she let on, while Liz's doubts about Vivien's reliability had been amply confirmed.

Emily removed the small manilla envelope from the dead-letter drop in the stables and ran her eyes over the messages that she would have to transmit. One in particular caught her eye and she frowned as she read:

'For urgent attention stop suspicions of Solange now intolerable stop she concealed unauthorized visit to Toulouse where sighted in company of German officers stop request her immediate recall . . .'

Emily had not finished reading when the latch on the stable door clicked and the door slowly opened. It was

Vivien, carrying a small attaché case which contained one of Emily's new transmitters.

Vivien chattered brightly as Emily checked that her new wireless was in order. But for the first time in their relationship Emily was wary of the older woman. When Vivien asked whether she had found a new safe house, she held back from telling her friend where it was.

Emily had snapped the case shut and was about to leave when Vivien took her by the arm and looked her straight in the eye.

'What's the matter?' she asked.

'Nothing,' Emily lied unconvincingly.

Vivien looked at the messages which Emily was holding in her hand and asked her whether they contained some problem. Emily's expression gave the game away as she backed off from Vivien.

'You know I'm not allowed to show them to anyone, Solange,' Emily cried.

'Oh, for Pete's sake, Zoe, you've shown them to me often enough before!'

'This is different,' Emily said desperately.

'Why?' asked Vivien. Suddenly, the penny dropped. 'Is it about me?'

Emily pursed her lips. 'I can't say, Solange, I'm sorry.'

'Oh, don't be so damn ridiculous!' Vivien shouted. Snatching the sheet of paper out of Emily's hand, she leaned back against the stable door and looked down the list of messages. Quickly she came to the one which referred to her.

'Oh, Christ,' she muttered as she handed back the sheet of paper to Emily. 'So that's what Colette was on about.'

She glared at Emily. 'Did you tell her I'd been to Toulouse?'

Emily looked at her friend in horror.

'No, of course not. I've not told anyone – I swear it!'

Vivien looked puzzled. 'How did she know, then?'

The two women stood looking at each other silently. Emily was the first to speak.

'Is it true?' she asked, dreading the answer.

'What?'

'That you were with . . . German officers?'

'Course it's bloody true,' snapped Vivien bitterly. 'Yvette's gone and got herself a boy-friend in the Wehrmacht, the stupid girl!'

She clenched her fists and banged them violently against the stable door. 'God, what a mess!' she moaned.

'What will you do?' asked Emily quietly.

Vivien turned round and thought for a moment.

'Obviously, the sooner I come clean with Yvette, the better.'

'Wouldn't it be easier just to tell Colette the truth?'

'Not bloody likely! She'd probably have me shot!' Vivien laughed bitterly. 'I'm not giving up on Yvette now, Zoe – not when I've come so far.'

As she cycled down the track away from the château, Emily found herself admiring Vivien's persistence, but wondered whether it would be better all round if she broke her confidence and told Liz the truth. For the moment, however, she pushed such thoughts to the back of her mind and concentrated on reaching the remote barn from which she would transmit to London.

After she had sent her messages and hidden her new transmitter, she set off back to Montaud, wanting to pay one last visit to the Ferrier's shop. From a distance the town looked an idyllic place with its mediaeval walls rising out of the surrounding countryside.

Emily wheeled her bicycle cautiously through the cobbled streets until she came to the narrow road that led down to what once had been home. The shop was now boarded up and deserted. She was standing on the other side of the street, looking at it sadly, when a fat woman pushed by her.

Emily jumped out of the way and for a split second, the two women stared at each other. To Emily's horror, she found herself looking straight into Annette's face, but with a sickening sense of relief she realized that Annette did not recognize her in her new disguise.

Hurriedly Emily apologized and walked on. She was just about to turn the corner into the market square when she stopped and looked back. To her surprise, she saw Annette turning into the back entrance of the shop, so she retraced her steps and slipped up the alleyway to Leon's workshop. To her dismay, she saw Annette take down the ornate ormulu clock which had been Leon's pride and joy and place it carefully in her basket.

Unsure what to do, Emily considered confronting Annette and then thought better of it. With a horrible sense of powerlessness, she slipped away before the older woman caught sight of her.

Knowing that she had very little time left before she would return to England, Vivien went to Toulouse. To her intense disappointment, Yvette had once again arranged to go dancing with Jurgen.

'Why don't you come too?' Yvette suggested.

Once again Vivien found herself having to be charming to the loathsome Voller, who flattered her with heavy-handed compliments.

'I feel that I have met you before,' he said.

'I don't think so,' replied Vivien nervously.

Later, while the two women titivated themselves in

front of the mirror in the cloakroom, Vivien suggested to Yvette that she come and spend the next weekend at the château. To Vivien's great pleasure, the girl readily agreed; it seemed Jurgen was on duty, so she would be all on her own and at a loose end.

When they returned to their table, they found that Voller had ordered another bottle of champagne. More and more wine was drunk and the party became increasingly animated, but Vivien found it increasingly difficult to remain cheerful; the intensity with which Voller gazed at her was unsettling. Her mood was not improved when Yvette produced a camera and insisted on taking several group snaps. At first Vivien pretended to be camera-shy, but in the end she gave in. She knew she could not make too much of a fuss without drawing attention to herself.

Kit went straight round to Liz's safe house after his visit to the factory. As they studied the plans, he expressed his suspicions of Sylvestre.

'It was pretty damn clear that Sylvestre wasn't telling me the whole truth,' he said, indicating the guarded room on the plans.

'How do you mean?' Liz asked.

'Well, it's no auxiliary generator, that's for sure. Far too much security for that.'

'What is it then?'

'It's the main transformer for the whole plant.'

'Are you sure?'

'Positive,' Kit asserted. 'And that's not all. I'm certain the same transformer feeds the factory making ball-bearings next door.'

Liz thought about the implications of Kit's information for a moment.

'I see,' she mused.

'Exactly! Destroy the transformer and we put two plants out of action for the price of one!'

'That's terrific! So Sylvestre has been playing us along.'

'Yes. You can see why the Communists lump the capitalist class with the Germans. He'll get what he deserves.'

Liz was already thinking about the mission.

'Does this mean we're going to need more people?' she asked with a worried expression on her face.

'Probably, yes. The place is pretty well guarded.'

Liz frowned. 'Pity. I was hoping we could keep this one small scale.'

'I'm only talking about two or three extra men. Josef will be able to manage that.'

'He's not my main worry,' sighed Liz. Kit caught the sound of concern in her voice and looked at her questioningly.

'You have to know. We think Solange is a security risk. It's possible she's been compromised by the Germans.'

Kit gawped at her. 'I don't believe it!'

Liz shook her head. 'Yes. She must on no account be told anything about this operation. Absolutely nothing.'

Liz then offered to make Kit something to eat. She brought out a bottle of wine and gave it to him to open while she prepared an omelette.

'Do you know that's the first meal you've ever cooked me?' he said, looking fondly across the table at her as he wiped the plate clean with a piece of bread.

Liz got up from her chair and started to clear away the dishes.

'Is it? I've always been pretty hopeless in the kitchen – probably because mother was so good.'

'Well,' said Kit, leaning back in his chair, 'it's the best omelette I've ever tasted.'

He poured himself another glass of wine and studied Liz as he stood by the window, looking out on the street below. Abruptly she turned and told him he should be on his way. Kit looked at Liz with disappointment.

'I could stay the night.'

Liz turned on him.

'No,' she said firmly. 'It's too dangerous, and you know it.'

He pushed back his chair and went across the room towards her.

'Oh, come on Liz . . .'

He was taken aback by the force of her response.

'You know as well as I do, it's against every security rule in the book!'

'The rules never bothered you before.'

'It's different now. I'm leader.'

'Oh, I see. That makes you less human all of a sudden, does it?'

'Oh, for God's sake!' Liz snapped, then looked at Kit more gently. 'If you like, yes, it does.'

He grimaced. 'So that's it, is it?'

'Yes, that's it. Kit, we agreed in England it was over.'

'Did we?'

'Yes, and this is neither the time nor the place to start it up again.'

'Oh.' Kit was considerably taken aback by Liz's officious manner. 'So when is it the time and the place, may I ask?'

Liz felt wretched. She would have given anything to fall into Kit's embrace, but she knew it was impossible.

'Kit, you're not making it any easier for either of us.'

'And you're not making any bloody sense! You went

back to Laurence out of duty. Now you're getting divorced from him . . .'

'And now I'm here. I have a job to do and so have you. We have no right to risk the lives of others by indulging ourselves.'

Kit stared at her hard, then turned and picked up his cap. Liz looked at him, full of apprehension that she had said too much.

'I'm sorry, but that's how it has to be,' she said softly.

Kit walked towards the door, where he stopped.

'I can see why they made you leader. You've changed.'

'The world has changed, Kit.'

'Victor,' Kit corrected her bitterly. 'Victor, remember? Victor, not Kit. That's the rule, isn't it?'

He left her apartment and pulled the door firmly shut. Liz bit her lip and closed her eyes. A leader doesn't cry, she told herself.

Emily parked her bicycle by the old covered market and stood inconspicuously by one of the pillars. The position gave her a good view down the road which led to the Ferriers' shop. She did not have to wait long before Annette came out of her house and walked up towards the market-place. Emily tailed her as she went about her morning's shopping, and began to wonder whether she was on a fool's errand.

Suddenly, Emily observed Annette look round furtively before disappearing up a side alley. She followed at a safe distance and watched with growing interest as Annette entered the lobby to a block of flats. About to follow Annette into the building, she looked at her watch and remembered that she had a sked in less than half an hour.

Her investigation of Annette would have to wait for another day.

Emily frowned as she decoded the message from London, debating whether to break Vivien's confidence and tell Liz about the visits to Toulouse. On the other hand, there did not seem much point. The instructions from London were very specific: Vivien was to be brought back to England.

Liz was already waiting for Vivien in the derelict barn, sitting on a bale of hay.

'I've had a message from London about you,' she said.

Vivien looked at her leader sharply.

'They want to recall you for retraining,' said Liz, 'as a wireless operator.'

Vivien looked at her in astonishment. 'You're joking!' she exclaimed.

Liz shook her head gravely. 'Message came in yesterday. What do you think?'

'I think it bloody stinks! I'm doing a job here, for God's sake.'

'I know, Solange, but they're desperately short of pianists at the moment.' She paused before continuing, 'And you have been out here some time; you deserve a break.'

'Like hell! Have you put them up to this?'

Liz looked at Vivien, tight-lipped.

'Of course not. You're a damn good courier and I'd hate to lose you . . .'

'But you wouldn't fight to keep me?'

'London has to have the final say.'

'You mean I have no choice? It's an order?'

'We're all under orders.'

Vivien wandered across the barn, as far away from Liz as possible. 'So when do I go?'

'As soon as they can arrange a flight to take you out.'

Vivien looked at Liz in horror . . .

Emily resumed her tailing of Annette. The older woman followed the same pattern as before and after a morning's shopping ended up at the same seedy block of flats.

This time, Emily did not have to dash off, but she made her way cautiously across the courtyard and past the empty concierge's kiosk. She had started to climb the stairs to the flats when she heard voices coming from just above her. Hurriedly looking round for somewhere to hide, she opened the nearest door on the half-landing and found herself in a very basic lavatory. She quickly fastened the door with its wire clasp and put her eye to a crack in the door through which she could just about see the landing above.

At first there seemed to be no one there, but just as she was about to unfasten the door and make a dash for it, she heard voices again. Through the crack in the door, she made out Annette on the landing above. She was talking to a man who spoke with a German accent and she was extremely agitated.

'I don't want to meet here again,' she muttered. 'Somebody might see us.'

The man nodded in agreement. 'All right. We'll make it the other place in Arbon.'

'Did you bring the money?' Annette asked greedily.

'Here.' The German handed her a wad of notes.

'Oh, thank you, Herr Voller.'

'You're doing rather well out of all this, aren't you?' Voller sneered. 'And I bet you've helped yourself to one or two items from the house too?'

Annette went on the defensive.

'We all have to get by, don't we? One way or another. I'd better go then. Have they found that girl yet? The one who escaped from the shop?'

'No, not yet.'

Annette was worried. 'She knows too much about me; she might put two and two together.'

'Don't worry, we shall catch her sooner or later.'

'It was her I was after, not Marie and Leon.'

'Oh?' Voller sounded sceptical.

'Marie was all right. Where is she now?'

Voller looked at the greedy old woman with disdain. 'Don't ask, woman. That is not your concern.'

Voller shut the door of the flat firmly in Annette's face and she stuffed the money into her handbag and set off down the stairs. On the half-landing, she tried to enter the lavatory where Emily was hiding and Emily gasped as the frail wire clasp almost snapped with the strain. But it held, and Annette swore in exasperation and went on down the stairs.

Emily waited for a few minutes before she let herself out of the lavatory and then made her way back to the Maquis hideout. She was surprised by Luc's reaction when she told him her news as they sat huddled over a small bonfire some distance from the other Maquisards. He sat calm and still after she finished speaking, gazing into the embers.

'She must die,' he said.

Emily looked at him.

'That's what we do with collaborators,' he explained.

'Yes, of course,' Emily nodded. She made a swift decision. 'Let me do it, Luc.'

'You?'

'It's my job. I owe it to them.'

He smiled slightly. 'Can you use a gun?'

Emily was annoyed by his patronizing attitude.

'Of course I can. I've probably had a damn sight more weapons training than you!'

Luc raised his hands in an ironically submissive gesture.

'I believe you – but you're sure you want to do this?'

Emily stared into the fire.

'Yes,' she said, trying to convince herself.

Yvette arrived by bus to spend the weekend with Vivien. Juliette was away and Vivien was almost beside herself with excitement at finally having the girl to herself.

As they made an extensive tour of the château and grounds, Yvette did not tell her new friend that she had slept with Jurgen the previous night and had boasted about Vivien living in a château. And of course, when Jurgen had asked for the address, Yvette had given it to him without a second thought. Why not?'

The two of them settled down for a chat in Vivien's bedroom, Yvette cradling her bowl of coffee as the pair of them sat side by side on the bed.

Vivien decided to confide in Yvette.

'I'm going to be leaving soon.'

Yvette looked at the older woman with surprise.

'Leaving?' she queried.

'Leaving France – maybe as early as next week.'

'But why? How?'

'Because I'm going back to England.'

'Yvette stared at Vivien in puzzlement. 'I don't understand . . .'

Before she could continue, Vivien interrupted.

'One of the reasons I came to France was to look for you, Yvette. I traced Father Giraud and through him located Marguerite, who told me where to find you in Toulouse. You see, I'm not Christine Rousset at all.'

'Who are you, then?' the girl demanded.

Vivien looked at her beseechingly.

'I'm your mother,' she said as quietly as possible.

Yvette simply gazed at her with complete incredulity.

'What?' she screeched.

Vivien grasped her by the hand.

'I'm English and my real name is Vivien Ashton. But years before the war I worked in Paris, where I met your father. He left me before you were born and Father Giraud persuaded me to have you adopted.'

Yvette abruptly withdrew her hand.

'I don't believe you!' she cried.

'I swear to you, I'm telling the truth.'

Yvette got up from the bed and backed away from her mother.

'I want you to come with me, Yvette. Back to England. It's possible I can get you out,' Vivien urged.

Yvette stared at Vivien angrily.

'If you really are my mother, you have a damn nerve! After all these years, you think you can just walk back into my life!'

Vivien stood up. 'Yvette!' she whispered.

Yvette stamped her foot, choking back the tears.

'Well, you can't! Do you hear? I don't want you! I hate you and I never want to see you ever again!'

The girl ran out of the room and Vivien rushed after her, but Yvette was too quick. She dashed downstairs and out of the front door, slamming it hard behind her. Stumbling down the front steps, brushing the tears from her face, she failed to see the car drawn up outside.

In front of her were four SD agents. Two took Yvette by the arms and led her away to a waiting black car, while the others went inside the château. They found Vivien in one of the bedrooms; she sat slumped and weeping, her fists rhythmically pounding the wall.

Annette's back door swung open as Emily pushed it, walking stealthily across the back yard to the lean-to conservatory at the back of the house. She rattled the handle on the french windows and called out for Annette. She knocked, and still there was no reply. Carefully she removed the gun from her bag and slipped into the house.

She walked very cautiously along a dingy corridor, stopping at the bottom of the stairs and calling out to Annette again. Silence pervaded the house. She opened a door and peered into the room. The curtains were drawn and a single table-lamp lit the room. With her back to the door was Annette, seated in a winged armchair.

Emily grasped her gun tightly, summoning up all her courage.

'Madame . . .' she began, advancing on Annette.

Puzzled by the lack of reply, she leaned forward and touched Annette on the shoulder. To her horror, the woman's head fell forward to reveal an ugly bullet wound in the back of the neck.

Emily moved round to stand in front of the woman and

gasped as she saw what had been done to her. Annette's hands were tied, her ankles roped to the chair. A sheet of paper with the word 'Collaborator' scrawled across it was pinned to her chest. The Maquis had got to her first. Emily turned away, sickened by the sight.

CHAPTER 7

It was a bright, cold November afternoon when Liz and Kit reconnoitred Sylvestre's factory with Josef. The three of them lay on their stomachs in the long grass, on a hill overlooking the plant. Smoke from the factory chimneys spiralled slowly up into the sky. Josef passed the binoculars to Liz, who studied the signs of activity below.

A podgy German sentry lounged in his sentry-box, while another guard sat outside on an oil-drum smoking a cheroot in the thin sun. Liz was pleased to see that the human security was not very formidable – guard duty here appeared to be a soft option for middle-aged men. The physical security of the factory seemed much more daunting, since the whole place was surrounded by a chain-link fence topped with barbed wire.

Josef filled them in on the details.

'They have only six men on duty at any one time. And at night, three patrol while three sleep. They do two hours on, two off in rotation.'

'Where do they sleep?' asked Liz, panning along the perimeter fence with the binoculars.

'There.' Josef leaned over and moved Liz's hand to the correct position. 'Over by the gate. They have a small guard-house. That's where their phone is, it's a direct line to Arbon – it has to be cut first of all.'

Liz followed the telegraph wire from the guard-house up to a pole by the perimeter fence. Half a dozen wires radiated from the telegraph pole, making it impossible to work out which one came from the bunk-house. She passed the binoculars to Kit so that he could get a better look.

'Yes,' she said, 'But which wire? It looks like a cat's got at the knitting down there.'

Josef thought for a moment and suggested that they all go down and look at the pole more closely.

Liz gaped at him. 'Do you think that wise?' she asked.

Josef grinned and produced a basket full of odd-looking mushrooms.

'You can never tell how hot the fire is until you get up close,' he said cheerily, as he rose to his feet. The others looked curiously at the multi-coloured fungi.

'What the hell are those?' enquired Kit.

'Cepes and girolles,' Josef answered.

Liz wrinkled her nose. 'They look poisonous to me.'

'Not these,' replied the Frenchman. 'When you're hungry, you soon learn which is which.'

Liz picked a girolle out of the basket and held it up to look more closely at it. 'Remind me to tell Cad to add mushrooms to the training course,' she said to Kit as they followed Josef down the hillside towards the factory.

Liz and Josef strolled alongside the factory fence with their eyes fixed on the ground, pretending to look for mushrooms, while Kit watched them from the hillside.

Josef muttered out of the corner of his mouth to Liz, 'Let me do the talking.'

Liz nodded in agreement as they approached the main gates. The sentry sitting on the oil-drum looked up and ambled over.

'Hey!' he shouted. 'You there! What're you doing?'

Josef looked at the man in surprise. 'Who? Us?'

'Yes, you!' the guard shouted, 'Come here!'

Josef went up to the fence and held up his basket of mushrooms.

'Mushrooms,' he explained. 'The region's famous for them. You want to buy some? They're very good fried with just a little garlic.'

While he embarked on an elaborate game of bartering with the guard, Liz tested the base of the fence with her foot and studied the telegraph pole and its wires more closely.

When Josef thought he had strung out his conversation for as long as he could, a deal was struck and the guard went back to his post, well pleased with his purchase.

'I think we really must put mushroom identification on the course,' said Liz as they walked away from the factory. 'We could have had a walkover tomorrow night.'

Josef looked at her curiously.

'Well, we've just passed up a God-given opportunity to poison the whole lot of them!'

Josef laughed and suddenly Liz felt much more confident about the whole enterprise. He suggested that they go to the Maquis hideout to discuss further plans, which was considerable progress from the time when Liz had had to winkle every bit of information out of him. And she was glad of the opportunity to make sure that Emily was all right.

Up in the ruined farmhouse, Luc and Emily joined in the discussion about the forthcoming raid. Luc produced a bottle of wine which they all sipped as they studied the plans of the factory.

Emily volunteered to cut the telephone wires with a

little assistance from Luc. Liz registered with slight concern the way the two young people looked at each other; there seemed to be rather more than a comradely bond between them.

'We need a signal when they're cut,' said Liz, returning to the matter in hand.

'Flashlight,' stated Luc. 'One long flash if they're cut, and three times if there's a problem.'

'We'll have to smuggle all our stuff into the factory beforehand,' put in Kit. 'I don't fancy playing Santa Claus with thirty pounds of plastic explosive on my back.'

Liz had a simple solution. The man who collected the rubbish could take the explosives in. They would be hidden in a bin by the main gate, ready for use when Kit and Liz had cut through the fence and got into the factory.

Josef outlined his plan to create a diversion to draw away the guards so that they could get to the transformer, their main target, as quickly as possible. He was concerned that the entire operation should last no longer than fifteen minutes. Even with the telephone wires down, the sound of gunfire would bring reinforcements from Arbòn.

For their getaway, a stolen timber lorry would be hidden on the edge of the nearby woods, a couple of hundred yards from the factory.

After they had run through the timetable from start to finish, Liz looked round at each member of the team.

'You all realize just how important this is, don't you?' she said seriously. 'We can't afford to fail. This is one operation which has to go like a Swiss watch.'

Josef smiled at her.

'Don't worry,' he said. 'This will be like Bastille day, but with better fireworks!'

Emily asked whether they should warn Vivien and Liz shook her head emphatically. On no account was she to be told anything; everyone was ordered to stay away from the château.

Liz then asked the question which was nagging everyone. Could they trust Sylvestre?

'He knows the consequences if he opens his mouth,' said Josef gravely, drawing his finger across his neck to demonstrate.

Deep inside the SD headquarters in Arbon, Vivien and Yvette shared a cell. The small room was filthy and covered in graffiti; the only furniture was two narrow iron beds and a chamber-pot. Tired and dishevelled, the two women sat on their beds and dunked grey bread into tin bowls of coffee. Yvette looked at her mother resentfully and asked what she thought the SD would do to them.

Vivien sighed. 'What can they do to us?' she asked rhetorically. 'I'm just a mother looking for her lost child. That is all I'm guilty of.'

Vivien put her bowl down on the floor and went to sit next to Yvette. She put her arms round her daughter's shoulders and started to stroke her hair, but Yvette pushed her hand away abruptly.

'Don't be stupid!' she snapped. 'Look at us! Just look at us! Don't you realize who these people are?'

Vivien looked saddened by this outburst.

'Why did you have to come and mess around with my life like this?' cried the girl. 'Everything was fine until you came along! Why couldn't you have left me alone!'

'Because you're my daughter, Yvette. Can't you understand that? They can't shoot me for loving you, can they?'

Yvette looked at her mother pityingly. 'There are

plenty of Frenchmen who'd shoot *me* for loving a German.'

Suddenly the cell door opened and two men in uniform appeared. Vivien recognized one of them as Voller's man, Schnabel. He ordered Vivien out of the cell. She rose slowly from the bed and looked back to see Yvette crouched and covering her face with her hands.

Vivien was hustled down the corridor to a bare interrogation room where a large picture of Hitler hung high up on the wall. She sat down on a chair opposite Voller, who was flipping through a pile of papers in front of him. The guard and Schnabel remained standing by the door.

Voller put down Vivien's ID, *Livret de Famille* and the group photograph that Yvette had taken, and stared hard at her.

'Who are you, Madame?' he asked sardonically. 'Are you the charming Christine Rousset of the tea dance? Are you Solange Françoise Augier, of sixteen Rue du Bac, Rouen? Or are you somebody else altogether?'

Vivien clenched her fists and stared straight ahead of her.

'My name is Augier,' she said, 'I decided to use a false name when I started to look for . . .'

Voller sighed irritably. 'Your daughter. So you said before.'

He scrutinized Vivien carefully and then looked down at the documents. 'It says here that you are a children's nurse by profession.'

Vivien nodded. 'That's correct.'

'I understand you were a nurse in the Red Cross and that you took part in the Great War?'

'Yes. I was seventeen.' Vivien could recount her cover story in her sleep. 'I spent one year in a hospital near

Verdun and then I went to Salle Petriaire Hospital in Paris at the end of the war, nursing amputees.'

Voller looked coldly at her. 'Do you believe in life after death, Madame Augier?' he asked.

Vivien looked at him strangely, anxiety gnawing at her. What had he found wrong with her documents?

'What?' Vivien asked and then thought for a moment before replying. 'Yes, I do.'

'Do you believe in reincarnation?'

She paused again and looked at her inquisitor.

'Why are my religious beliefs so important to you?'

'Because I have to satisfy myself that you have returned from the dead. You see, Madame . . .' Voller held up a document that looked like a military record sheet, 'Solange Françoise Augier, according to her record, was killed by shellfire on the second of June 1917 – while serving at the Hospital at La Grange, three miles from the front.'

Vivien protested. 'That's ridiculous! I've never even heard of La Grange. I worked at the Salle Petriaire after Verdun.'

Voller smiled a thin smile.

'Madame, it's not for me to decide who is right or who is wrong. I am under orders to sent you to Bordeaux, where we have a special department which deals with resurrections. I am sure that they will be delighted to investigate this miracle.'

Vivien's face paled.

'Please Monsieur, I beg you,' she pleaded. 'It's all a great mistake. I was never at this La Grange place; I don't even know where it is.'

'I doubt you know where Verdun is either,' Voller snapped as he waved to the guard to remove Vivien.

Vivien struggled as the guard grabbed her by the arms and pulled her from the chair.

'Please, Monsieur . . .' she cried as the man dragged her from the office.

Vivien was in turmoil as she was manhandled back to her cell. What was she to tell Yvette, who already seemed so close to breaking point? Vivien knew that the interrogation process had hardly started, and that the strongest agents found it hard not to break. What would these people do to Yvette?

As soon as she was pushed through the cell door, Yvette demanded to know what happened. Vivien forced herself to smile and embraced the girl.

'I told you it would turn out all right, didn't I? They're just sending us to Bordeaux for a few more questions, then we can leave.'

Yvette gave a huge sigh of relief and sank back on her bed.

'Thank God for that!' she exclaimed.

Vivien turned away from her daughter.

'Yes, my darling. We'll soon be free.'

Tears welled up in her eyes and she tried hard to blink them back, but they kept on coming. She couldn't bear to think how it would all end.

Schnabel was annoyed to discover that there were no cars available to take Voller and the women to Gestapo headquarters in Bordeaux the next day. Felix, the chief mechanic, slowly rubbed his thick pebble glasses and gazed round the garage, shaking his head. All fifteen cars belonging to the SD motor pool were out of commission. Finally, Felix pointed to the lorry which he had been working on.

'He can have this lorry, if he wants.'

'A lorry?' said Schnabel. 'He doesn't want a lorry.

We're transporting ladies, Felix, not Jews. When can he have one?'

'Day after tomorrow with a bit of luck. What is it?' Felix winked at Schnabel. 'Business or pleasure?'

Schnabel leaned against one of the cars and lit a cigarette. 'A bit of both,' he said with an unpleasant smile. 'We're taking a Madame Solange Augier for a physical examination.'

Felix wrinkled his nose. 'For a what?'

'A physical,' said Schnabel impatiently. 'You know, tubes, water . . . It's a damn sight more entertaining than sticking your hands inside that bloody thing.'

Schnabel got up and walked towards the garage door.

'Day after tomorrow then, Felix, and make sure it's got a full tank!'

Felix returned to work on the lorry. At lunch-time, he left the garage and instead of going to his usual café, crossed town and visited one by the bus station. To his relief, there were no customers standing at the bar as he approached it. He ordered a glass of peppermint and then leaned across the counter.

'Got a light, Phillipe?' he asked the portly patron, Rodez, who was busy wiping glasses.

Rodez glanced round the café and passed over a box of matches. Felix quickly removed a match and slipped a tiny folded note inside the box, sliding the cover shut. Then he lit his cigarette and casually handed the box back to Rodez. Downing his drink in one gulp, Felix slipped out of the bar. As soon as he was out of sight, Rodez picked up the phone by the bar counter and dialled a number.

Maison Sylvestre was a small château with rather too

well manicured gardens for wartime. Liz walked with Sylvestre between the immaculately trimmed box parterres as she told him the Resistance's plan to blow up the transformer room.

'It was installed by German engineers from Siemans,' she told the factory owner. 'It is helping their war effort, whether you like it or not . . .'

'And what about my efforts to keep the place open?' he pleaded. 'What about the people who work there? Do you know what could happen to them? They could all finish up doing slave labour in Germany.'

'Most of your work force are old people, Monsieur Sylvestre. They wouldn't send them to Germany.'

'Age is of no concern to the Germans, only labour. Do you know, Mademoiselle, I built that factory with my own hands? And now you want to destroy it!'

Liz looked hard at him.

'There is a war going on, Monsieur Sylvestre.'

The man glared at Liz.

'War? What do you know about war?' he snapped. He took out his wallet and pulled out a fading photograph of a smiling French soldier in First World War uniform, which he handed to Liz.

'Ask him about war, Mademoiselle,' he said bitterly. 'Maurice, my brother. He knows all about war. He's an expert. He was killed by it. Wherever there are the English, there is trouble. You mark my words!'

'We only want to put your factory out of action.'

'Sure. Put it out of action. Put me out of action. Put all of us out of action. Why don't you call in the RAF while you're at it and get it over with in one go?'

'Don't you want this war to end? Or are you just content with taking money from the Germans, like the Communists say? Is that all there is to it? Has it come down to this?'

Sylvestre reflected, but he was not going to answer her question. He held up his hands in a gesture of resignation.

'Do what you have to, Mademoiselle. But if there are reprisals or deportations, it will be on your shoulders. I just hope you can live with that.'

'And I hope that you can live with taking blood money from our enemies, Monsieur Sylvestre.'

Josef supervised the explosives as they were carefully transported from their places of concealment to the Maquis hide-out. He watched as Liz and Kit, slowly and methodically, rolled the plastic explosive into charges and placed them in a grubby corn-sack underneath the table. Then he pulled a key out of his pocket and handed it to Liz.

'This is a duplicate key to the transformer room,' he explained. 'The guard goes after they shut down the plant for the night.'

Liz took the key and told the men about her meeting with Sylvestre.

'He's got second thoughts about having his factory blown to bits. He gave me the hair shirt speech about reprisals and putting everybody out of work.'

Kit started to make the detonators. He measured the length of each fuse carefully and inserted it into a detonator. Gingerly he crimped the detonator over the fuse, which he then rolled up into a coil and placed carefully in a small metal ammunition case.

'He's bound to get cold feet before the event,' acknowledged Kit. 'We'll just have to warm them up for him, won't we?'

Kit, Liz and Josef watched anxiously as Pascal, the rubbish man, loaded the bin containing the old corn-sack on to his cart. As the horse pulled off down the rutted track into the gloom of the evening, Emily and Luc came cycling towards the farmhouse at full pelt.

Liz saw immediately that something was terribly wrong.

'Solange has been arrested by the Gestapo!' Emily gasped. 'They're transferring her to Bordeaux the day after tomorrow!'

Liz looked at all of them as they gathered round the farmhouse table.

'We know what's going to happen in Bordeaux,' she said. 'We can kiss the whole outfit goodbye if they get their hands on her.'

She looked round the gathering. 'Is there no way we can get them out of there?'

Josef shook his head.

'It takes time, Colette, and that's one thing we don't have just now.'

Liz felt at her wits' end. Emily had finally broken her promise to Vivien and revealed the truth about the trips to Toulouse.

'If it wasn't for her daughter, she might have held out for a few days – weeks, even. Right now, I'd give her forty-eight hours at the most. The only bonus is that she knows nothing about the factory job.'

The solution that Kit suggested was to ambush the German car on it's way to Bordeaux. Lix looked sceptical, but Josef nodded in approval and explained how he had organized a successful attack on the road running through the Forest of Dirac. Liz looked round at everyone for agreement.

'That settles it. We go for an ambush the day after the raid.' She was surprised to see Kit frowning slightly.

'Do you agree, Victor?' she asked.

'It's your show, Colette,' he said half-heartedly.

'What other alternative do we have?' Liz turned to him.

Kit leaned back in his chair.

'We could always mine the road,' he said softly. 'We've got fifteen pounds of PE left. Surprising what that stuff can do to a car.'

Liz stared at him in amazement. 'She's on our side,' she said angrily.

'You mean we *hope* she is,' he pointed out.

Liz asserted her authority and told Kit that Vivien was going back to England alive, and with her daughter. Emily was ordered to get on to London and ask for a plane to be put on standby; it was to leave the moment that they knew Vivien was on her way to Bordeaux, and to use the landing strip at Touzac.

At Baker Street, Emily's message reduced Cad to a rage.

'Who the bloody hell do they think I am?' he shouted at Faith. 'Chief of the Air Staff? What's going on down there? Why can't they get her out through Spain?'

Faith tried to calm him down, but mentioning Vivien's daughter only sent him into a further spin. He pounded up and down the office, stopping in front of his large-scale map of France. He jabbed his finger at Touzac.

'Just look where it is!' he shouted. 'Touzac's at about the limit of a Lysander's range. How the hell do they expect him to get down there?'

Faith tried to placate Cad. 'I've checked already. They can do it, but only with extra fuel tanks . . . and they think they can only bring one person out.'

Cad glared at Faith and relented. He told her to organize it.

It was early morning when Pascal arrived at the factory to collect the rubbish. Looking round carefully to see if anyone was watching, he placed the bin full of explosives next to two empty bins by the main gate. Having checked that the sack was covered by an old newspaper, he shut the lid.

As soon as Pascal had disappeared, Sylvestre emerged from behind a pile of crates where he had been hiding. He strolled through his deserted factory as if he were saying farewell to it. Pausing for a moment in front of the piles of spares waiting to be sent to Germany, he looked at them sadly.

Suddenly he clenched his fists and walked to the rubbish bins. Carefully, he removed the newspaper at the top and tossed it on the ground; then very gingerly he opened the sack. Lying on top of the explosives was the ammunition case containing the detonators and fuses. Sylvestre gently picked up the box and looked inside. He removed the detonators and stuffed them into his suit pockets; then he replaced the case on top of the explosives and closed the sack. Having made sure that everything looked as it had before, he went back into his factory. There was a faint smile of satisfaction on his face.

Later that evening, as the team lay in wait in the woody hill overlooking the factory, Liz gave them all a final briefing.

Josef looked like a Mexican revolutionary, festooned with magazine pouches and carrying a sten-gun. He was accompanied by six other members of the Maquis, all similarly dressed; they would provide the necessary diversion. Liz and Kit carried hunting bags with pistols strapped to their wrists. Luc flashed the torch, to check that it worked.

They all synchronized watches and Luc and Emily slipped away into the darkness towards the factory while Josef and his men moved off to approach the building from the rear, leaving only Kit and Liz lying in the undergrowth. Kit saw Liz trembling slightly as she checked for the umpteenth time that she had her wire-cutters. He leaned across and patted her on her arm.

She looked up at him through the darkness. 'I'm scared, Kit,' she confided.

'No, you're not,' he whispered back. 'You're excited. We're not sheep, you know. We wouldn't follow you if we didn't believe in you.'

She grinned slightly and nodded, trying to convince herself that he was right.

'Let's go,' she said, before any more doubts could emerge, and they started to crawl over the brow of the hill and down into the valley.

Silence reigned over the factory. The only light came from a dim bulb in the bunk-house, where the two half-dressed guards slept fitfully. Outside, a solitary guard stood silhouetted against the night sky, idly puffing on his cigarette.

Luc and Emily crept through the undergrowth up to the telegraph pole. Stealthily, Emily climbed the post and produced a pair of wire-cutters. She held the wires in one hand and squeezed on the cutters with the other, but nothing happened. Grunting with the effort, she tried again.

Luc looked up from the base of the pole. 'What's the matter?' he whispered.

'They won't work,' she hissed crossly.

Luc started climbing up to join her, but just then Emily squeezed with all her might and the wires went pinging into the air like whips. As soon as she had reached the ground, Luc took out the torch and flashed it once in the direction where Josef was hiding.

Seeing the light, Josef cocked his sten-gun as a signal for his men to do the same. There were six metallic rasps in the darkness.

'Right,' whispered Josef. 'Let 'em have it!'

Automatic gunfire erupted along the rear fence of the factory, drawing the guards away from the entrance. Under cover of the firing, Kit started to cut through the perimeter fence.

Inside the bunk-house, the two guards leapt out of their cots at the sound of the gunfire. One of them picked up the field telephone and wound it for all he was worth before he realized that the line had been cut. Then he slammed it back on the table in fury. The pair seized their rifles and ran out into the darkness.

The fence was nearly cut through when the two guards rushed past Kit and Liz. As soon as they had gone, Liz held open the gap to let Kit through. Once on the other side, he did the same for her and they ran towards the main building.

The sound of gunfire diminished once they were inside the factory. Kit removed the torch from his bag and shone it around, looking for the dustbins. As planned, the bins were situated by the door and they both hurriedly tipped the contents out on to the floor.

The sack was in Liz's bin. 'It's here!' she called excitedly.

Kit grabbed the sack and humped it towards the transformer room. Liz opened the door, and they stood on the threshold for a moment as he shone his torch over the array of dials and switches. He reached inside the sack to lift out the ammunition case and frowned. It felt very light. . . . He ripped off the top and stared into the box in disbelief.

'Well, well,' he said very calmly. 'We've been nobbled.'

'What do you mean?' she asked.

'Looks like Sylvestre really had got cold feet after all! Not a detonator in sight – not a time pencil between us.'

Liz groaned. 'What the hell do we do now?'

Kit looked at her grimly. 'Go home with our tails between our legs, I suppose.'

Another burst of gunfire echoed through the factory and Liz was filled with resolve.

'We're not going to be beaten this time, Kit.'

Kit looked at her for a moment and then rummaged in his bag, bringing out a hand grenade and a ball of string. The Outfit's training taught one to improvize.

'There were some oxygen cylinders out there. Bring them in here,' he told Liz. 'Get anything that will burn – petrol, paint, anything. I'm going to show Monsieur Sylvestre one gunpowder plot he'll never forget.'

Kit proceeded to tie the hand grenade to the transformer controls, as Liz went back into the workshop and began to pull the trolley containing the cylinders across the factory floor.

Josef started to get worried as time ticked by and still there was no sign of Kit and Liz. He and his men had very little ammunition left.

As Luc and Emily made their way back to the waiting lorry, one of the guards sped out of the factory gates on a motor-cycle and roared up the road towards Arbon. Luc rushed out into the middle of the road and fired his sten-gun as the motor-bike drove straight towards him. The machine kept on coming and he hammered away several more rounds.

The motor-bike was nearly on top of Luc when it veered off the road into a ditch where it burst into flames.

Luc shook his fist and shouted at the dead guard, 'That's for my mother, you bastard!'

He rejoined Emily and they ran back to the getaway vehicle, climbing up into the cab of the lorry. As they waited anxiously, Luc slid his arm round Emily and kissed her, but she was too worried about what was going on inside the factory to respond with any enthusiasm.

Meanwhile, Kit secured the grenade to the switching gear in the transformer room and smothered it with plastic explosive, spoiling the little 'sausages' which he and Liz had so carefully made. The oxygen cylinders were positioned so that they touched the plastic.

Kit winked at Liz. 'I wouldn't like to be around when this thing blows! Find any petrol?'

Liz looked at her watch. 'We've only got five minutes left. There's a drum of something out there.'

Kit nodded. 'Let's get a move on, then.'

Together they rolled a drum of petrol into place next to the oxygen cylinders.

'Right, that's it,' muttered Kit. 'Now, Colette, I want you to leave – get back to Josef.'

'I'm not going anywhere,' Liz insisted.

'What I'm about to do next could send this lot up. At least one of us should be around to tell the tale.'

'I'm staying,' she insisted.

Kit looked at her with a mixture of admiration and despair.

'OK, then, have it your own way. Find me a tin of paint or something which will burn.'

While Liz searched for the paint, Kit tied the end of the string to the ring of the grenade pin and then ran it out through the lock on the door. Liz returned with some cleaning fluid which she poured on the floor and Kit gingerly removed the pin from the grenade, until it was hardly holding down the lever.

'Set it alight!' Kit shouted, and they ran out of the transformer room. He shut the door and pulled the string as tight as he dared through the keyhole, then fixed it to the handle.

Turning to Liz, he grinned.

'Let's go.'

They turned on their heels and ran for the main gates. Leaving the building, they crouched down and dashed towards the gap they had made in the perimeter fence. They could still hear shooting as they crawled through the opening and made their way up to Josef.

'About bloody time!' shouted Josef, more in relief at seeing them than in anger.

He whistled and the firing stopped. Just as they turned to make for the woods, a German army lorry pulled up at the factory entrance; a dozen armed soldiers tumbled out and began to fan out round the perimeter fence.

Kit nudged Liz in the ribs. The first signs of fire could be seen glowing gently through the factory windows. Suddenly, the German's also saw the fire and rushed towards the building, trying to organize themselves into a fire-fighting team.

'Keep your heads down!' urged Kit.

As they all ducked, a huge ear-shattering explosion

came from deep within the factory and a great ball of flame erupted into the night sky. Windows blew out . . . doors flew into the air like giant splinters . . . the German soldiers were tossed up into the sky like rag-dolls.

The team stood and looked in amazement. They could scarcely believe their eyes – the roof of the factory had disappeared.

Liz gasped, 'Good God!' and turned to see Kit grinning from ear to ear. He grabbed her by the hand and they dashed off through the trees to the waiting lorry.

The celebrations at the Maquis hide-out went on until dawn.

The next day, rather the worse for wear, Kit and Liz cycled over to the site where they stood outside the factory gates with a number of other curious onlookers. Smoke still rose from the shell of the building as a few German soldiers half-heartedly sprayed hoses on the smouldering wreckage.

Liz turned to Kit in excitement, but he signalled that they should separate themselves from the crowd and they pushed their bicycles further along the road.

She whispered her pleasure to Kit: 'The place is a write-off!'

He grinned back. 'Isn't it just? Looks like it's been hit by a full load from a Wellie. I know someone who'll be checking his insurance policy this morning!'

Liz laughed. 'I hope he's kept his premiums up.'

Just at that moment, the crowds around the gate parted and a smart, expensive car nosed its way out of the factory. The vehicle accelerated to pass the cyclists, but slowed down as the driver recognized Kit and Liz.

Sylvestre wound down the car window; he looked like a broken man.

Liz smiled sweetly.

'Good morning, Monsieur Sylvestre. And how are you, this fine morning?'

'You bastards!' snarled Sylvestre.

Liz shook her head.

'You could quite easily have done it our way. We gave you the choice, but you just couldn't help yourself, could you?'

The Frenchman looked at them bitterly. 'You've ruined me!'

Kit shoved his head through the car window and spoke to Sylvestre.

'Destruction and rebuilding go hand in hand – that's progress. I'm sure something will rise out of the ashes.'

'How can you justify what you've done?'

Liz rounded on him. 'Quite easily, Monsieur. Righteous indignation, righteous indignation!'

As Sylvestre's car roared off down the road. Kit and Liz smiled somewhat bleakly at each other.

At SD headquarters, Vivien was close to despair. Yvette was continually moaning that they had been forgotten and Vivien only wished this was true.

'At least they're feeding us twice a day,' she said in an attempt to calm down her daughter.

Yvette stood on tiptoe, staring out of the cell window into the airless courtyard below. She gripped hard on to the cell bars.

'I don't care a damn about that! All I want to do is to get out of here!'

'What shall we do when they let us go?'

Yvette lowered herself down and turned round to face her mother.

'Let *me* go, you mean, don't you?'

Vivien hung her head. 'Oh, Yvette . . .' she sighed.

The cell door opened and Schnabel poked his head inside. He pointed at Vivien.

'Come on! You've got a visitor.'

Vivien bent over Yvette and kissed her on the cheek.

'You see, darling,' she said. 'They haven't forgotten us, after all.'

When she was ushered into the interrogation room where Voller had questioned her earlier, she saw to her surprise that Juliette was sitting at the far side of the table. Schnabel indicated to her that she was to sit opposite her old friend. He took a chair by the door to observe the encounter.

It was immediately obvious to Vivien that something was very wrong and that Juliette was putting a brave face on things. She looked sorrowfully at Vivien as she sat down.

'This is terrible, Solange,' she murmured. 'How on earth did you get yourself into this mess?'

Vivien tried to look confident.

'It'll sort itself out. They're sending us to Bordeaux.'

Juliette leaned forward, clasping both hands together on the table.

'Is there anything you want?' She asked tentatively. 'Is there anything I can get you?'

A flash of the old Vivien returned.

'You could bake me a cake and put a file inside it, I suppose,' she said, trying to sound nonchalant.

Juliette glanced across the room to Schnabel and lowered her voice still further.

'Is there anyone . . . you know what I'm trying to say.

Is there anyone you'd like me to speak to? Deliver a message to?'

Schnabel snapped at her to stop whispering as Vivien shook her head and asked how the baby was.

Juliette was nearly in tears. 'She misses you very much.' She bit her lip and pressed on with the same question.

'Are you *sure* that you don't want me to contact anyone?'

A tear rolled down Juliette's face and Vivien understood that she was acting under duress. She leaned across the table and put her hand over Juliette's to comfort her.

'It's all right, Juliette. I understand.'

The guard screamed at them not to touch each other and Juliette jerked her hands back and stood up, unable to contain herself any longer. Tears streamed down her face as she walked across the room, pausing for a moment by the door.

'Goodbye, Solange. God bless you!'

The guard hustled Juliette along the corridor to Voller's office, where he was sitting at his desk watching Juliette's baby play happily with his rubber stamps and pencils. A look of intense cruelty crossed his face as Juliette entered the room.

'Such a beautiful baby you have, Madame de Tramaut,' he purred. 'She'll grow up into a fine lady like her mother.'

Juliette reached out for the child, but the guard held her back. Tears cascaded down Juliette's cheeks.

'Give her back to me! Please give her back to me!'

Voller studied her face closely.

'How was Madame Augier? Didn't she have anything to say? Remember our little arrangement, Madame de Tramaut? Did you ask her what I told you?'

On the verge of collapse, Juliette stammered tearfully that she had asked the question twice and that Vivien had said there was no one.

Voller smiled coldly at the distraught woman.

'I hope for your child's sake that you are telling the truth; the world is never very kind to orphans.'

He then gestured to Juliette to take her child and she ran across the room to pick her up, hugging the baby close to her breast as she left the room.

'Motherhood and truth. For once, how well they go together. Organize the transport.' Voller's ominous words lingered in Juliette's mind as she hurried out of the building.

Much against his better judgment, Felix arranged to meet Emily and Luc in the back room of Rodez's café.

The two young people questioned the mechanic in great detail about the journey to Bordeaux. The trip was scheduled for the following day and Felix could prolong the task of repairing the cars no longer, as the Germans were beginning to be suspicious of the delays.

Luc's pleasure at hearing that the route was through the Forest of Dirac was tempered by the discovery that the car containing Vivien and Yvette would be accompanied by a military escort: a Kubelwagen containing four soldiers.

Up at the farmhouse, Liz made preparations for the ambush. Certainly it all seemed straightforward in comparison with the attack on Sylvestre's factory. The explosives left over from that attack were to be used to mine the road where it went through a very dense part of the forest. Josef was to organize the plane landing at Touzac and provide a back-up of armed men in the woods. Liz's task was to obtain the getaway car.

Everything seemed fine until Josef voiced one of the doubts that were haunting them.

'There is just one thing,' he said, almost as an afterthought. 'What if Felix's information is wrong and there's more than a four-man escort? We could be in for a very rough ride. What do we do then?'

They all looked at Liz. She addressed her team solemnly.

'Let me put it this way. It's imperative that we get Solange away from the Gestapo. She and Yvette must be on that plane when it leaves. If we can't manage that . . .' She hesitated for a moment, unable to bring herself to say the words.

Emily looked surprised, but finished Liz's sentence: 'Solange must not get to Bordeaux. Is that what you're trying to say?'

Liz braced herself and continued. 'I'm sure Felix's information is correct. He's always been right in the past, and we've no reason to doubt him now. Solange and Yvette will be over the Atlantic by nightfall, and tomorrow morning they'll be sitting down to a bacon-and-egg breakfast.'

Emily was still worried for her friend when she got up to do her sked and the news that came back from London worried her even more. As she decoded the message, the clear text shone out at her: ONLY ONE PASSENGER. Vivien would not be able to take her daughter with her, after all.

Automatically, Emily tidied everything away and destroyed the pieces of paper she used for decoding. She hid her radio set and then set off to tell Liz the bad news, but by the time she had returned to the hide-out, Liz had left with Luc to arrange the getaway car. They had decided to pay a surprise visit to Monsieur Sylvestre.

A look of terror crossed Sylvestre's face when he opened his front door and found Liz standing on his doorstep.

'What the hell do you want?' he asked angrily.

Liz smiled. 'Well, actually, we'd like your car.'

He stared at her and Luc for a moment and started to babble. 'Just a minute,' he said. 'Don't move! Stay right where you are!'

As he went back inside his house, Luc looked anxiously at Liz and put one hand on his gun, but Sylvestre suddenly reappeared with a large jerry-can full of petrol and his car keys. He handed the keys to Liz and the can to Luc.

'There, take it! Take it! You've taken everything else, you may as well take the rest. But just one thing, Mademoiselle – I never want to see you, or your friends, or the car ever again! Now please leave!'

With that outburst, he went back into the house and slammed the door.

Luc grinned at Liz and waved the petrol can aloft in celebration. Liz hoped this wasn't premature.

It was a fine day for the journey to Bordeaux and Vivien and Yvette blinked at the brightness of the winter sunshine as they were led out into the prison yard. A large black Citröen and a grey Kubelwagen containing four armed men were waiting.

Voller greeted the women with a sinister smile and held the back door of the Citröen open for them. Yvette looked at the Kubelwagen and the soldiers in surprise, then turned to Voller.

'I thought we were just going to Bordeaux for a few more questions?'

He smirked. 'But you are, Mademoiselle, you are. The men are going along for your own protection. These are dangerous times, as I'm sure you've realized.

Voller then clicked his fingers to one of the guards, who came forward with two pairs of handcuffs.

'You lied to me,' Yvette snarled at Vivien, as they both held out their arms to be fettered.

'Now, if you'd kindly get into the car, please?'

Voller spoke solicitously to the women, as if he was taking them to a social engagement. The Citröen followed the Kubelwagen out of the yard, with Voller sitting in the back alongside Vivien and Yvette.

The pines of the Dirac Forest stretched for miles and miles across the flat sandy soil of Les Landes. The whole countryside was permeated by the thick sticky smell of the pine trees.

Kit and Josef shivered slightly in the cold winter air as they set to work on their chosen piece of road. They were dressed as road repair men and, to give the whole operation an authentic look, a couple of road signs were positioned on either side of their hole. Two armed members of the Maquis stood guard as Kit's bomb was placed in position; the pair hummed as they filled in the hole with gravel. To complete the device, Kit ran the fuse-wire from the hole, across the road and into the forest. He laid the end of the wire next to a car battery before taking up a position which gave him a good view of the road and the hole.

Luc and the Maquisards also set up a caltrops: a device which when activated would puncture car tyres.

Emily found Liz waiting in Sylvestre's car, which was parked on a small track leading from the main road.

'I have to talk to you, Colette,' said Emily anxiously as she watched Liz load her small revolver.

'Why, what's the matter?' asked Liz automatically.

She was too preoccupied with her weapon to pick up the anxiety in Emily's voice as the girl continued.

'The message from London, confirming that the plane has left . . .'

'What about it?'

Liz looked at Emily in dismay as the girl told her that the plane could only take one passenger, but before they could discuss the matter further a shrill whistle from the Maquis lookout warned them that the Kubelwagen was approaching.

Liz and Emily ran to their stations.

'What are we going to do?' Emily asked breathlessly.

Gritting her teeth, Liz muttered that she didn't bloody well know. The women joined the others and lay down in the undergrowth at the roadside, watching like mesmerized rabbits as the convoy came down the road towards them. The Citröen travelled about ten yards behind the Kubelwagen.

From his vantage point, Kit watched intently as the vehicles drew nearer. One wire was securely tied to one of the battery terminals; the other he held in his hand. Immediately the German jeep was directly over the mine, Kit touched the battery terminal with the wire he was holding.

An explosion lifted the vehicle right up off the ground,

scattering pieces of bodywork and people everywhere. The remains landed with a crash and burst into flames – there couldn't possibly be any survivors.

The Citröen slammed on its brakes and started to reverse. It drove straight over the metal hooks of the caltrops, which caused the two back tyres to explode. The team dashed out of the trees towards the car as one of the guards opened fire.

Josef rushed up to the car and fired his sten-gun at the driver and the Gestapo guard. Bespattered by their blood, Yvette burst into hysterics and banged her fists on the car window.

Quickly assessing the situation, Voller raised his gun and held it to Yvette's temple. With his other hand, he took firm hold of the girl.

Josef tore open one of the back doors of the car, while Luc opened the other.

'Get out!' shouted Josef. 'Get out unless you want to end up in a war grave!'

Voller looked at Josef coldly and remained seated.

'Come on!' Liz shouted at Vivien and Yvette. 'Both of you get out quickly!'

Voller looked out of the car at his captors.

'Why don't we all take our time, Mademoiselle?' he said with a sneer. 'Nice and steady, no need for any more slaughter.'

Vivien spoke out as Yvette turned white. 'Do as he says, Colette! For God's sake, do as he says!'

'Why don't we all get out of the car?' Voller spoke quietly but with confidence as he eased Yvette out of the car, still holding the gun to her head.

'Now, the young lady and I are going to take a walk in the forest.

Everyone stood helpless as Voller pulled his victim

towards the trees. They had reached the edge of the road when suddenly Yvette called for help.

'Mummy! Mummy!' she howled. 'Please help me!'

For the first time in her life Vivien had been called 'Mummy', and her whole face changed expression. Growling at Voller like an animal, she threw herself at him and he staggered backwards and let go of Yvette. As he stumbled, his pistol went off, shooting the girl through the chest. Yvette dropped to the ground like a stone and in one leap, Vivien crouched over her daughter.

Voller raised his gun and pointed it directly at Vivien, but before he had time to pull the trigger Luc opened fire on the German with his sten-gun. Emily stood appalled at the carnage.

Liz stepped over Voller, who lay face down on the ground, and tried to wrench Vivien away from Yvette. Viven looked up from the body and glared at Liz.

'Get away from me!' she screamed. 'Get away from my baby! I hate you! I hate you all! Leave my baby alone . . .'

Liz looked down at the girl's body on the ground. There was no possibility that Yvette could be alive.

'She's dead, Solange!' she said quietly. 'There's nothing more anybody can do for her. Please, we've got a plane waiting to take you home. Please come now.'

For the first time since they had been in France, Liz used Vivien's real name. 'Vivien, please leave her!'

She knelt down next to the wailing woman and tried to take her hand, but Vivien pushed it roughly aside as she cradled Yvette's head in her arms.

'Leave her?' Vivien murmured crazily. 'You want me to leave her? I can't just leave my baby, just lying here. What kind of mother do you think I am?'

Liz looked aghast as Vivien started rocking Yvette

backwards and forwards, singing to her. She found herself on the verge of tears as Emily came up to try and help.

Emily crouched down next to Vivien and pleaded with her to come with them to the plane, but Vivien ignored her old friend and continued singing a lullaby to the dead girl.

Suddenly they all froze as a whistle came from further up the road. It was the signal that more Germans were approaching. Josef came across to Liz and told her that they would have to get going.

Liz stood up and pointed her gun at Vivien, looking at her angrily.

'If you don't get up right now and come with us, you'll never get up again!' she threatened. 'Come on! That's an order! On your feet!'

She and Emily tried once again to drag Vivien up on to her feet, but she clung even more fiercely to Yvette, looking up into Liz's face and laughing at her. The two women let Vivien go; there was nothing anyone could do for her. A look of madness suddenly crossed Vivien's face and she screamed at Liz.

'Go on, do it! Pull the trigger! Show us who's got the balls round here! Do it! Do it, you bitch!'

A second whistle came from the woods and a distant rumble of traffic could be heard.

Liz raised her gun and looked Vivien straight in the face.

'I'll do it, Vivien!' she said gently. 'As God is my judge, I'll do it.'

Vivien looked at her like a wounded animal and whimpered, 'Please, Liz, don't take her away from me now. She needs me . . . she needs me.'

Liz closed her eyes and squeezed the trigger –

shooting Vivien through the chest and sending her toppling back over Yvette's body. Then she lowered her gun and began to sob.

Emily looked at the scene through her hands and turned away rapidly. She ran to the side of the road and vomited.

Kit grabbed hold of Liz's arm and propelled her towards the getaway car. Luc took hold of Emily, and together they raced up the track towards Sylvestre's vehicle.

The army lorry came into view as Kit dragged Liz out of sight into the trees. She paused for a moment to look back at the bodies of Vivien and Yvette lying across the road.

Luc had already started the car. As soon as Liz and Kit had climbed in the back, he slammed into gear and set off along the track through the forest. Liz turned round in her seat and kept looking at the body of Vivien until it disappeared from view.

It was dark by the time the car reached the landing strip at Touzac. Josef had three men ready with flares for the approaching aeroplane.

Liz and Kit got out and stood at the edge of the airstrip, waiting for the Lysander. Kit grasped Liz by the shoulders and looked at her intently.

'I think you should go home, Liz,' he said softly. 'My orders are to stay on.'

Liz shook her head slowly, as he continued. 'In any case, this group's all washed up. We'd have had to split up anyway.'

Liz thought for a moment and asked what would happen to Zoe. Kit looked down fondly at Liz and told her that she would go with Luc into the Pyrenees, where they needed a radio operator.

'I think she has more reason to stay than any of us,' he said ruefully.

Liz turned to look at Luc and Emily. They were standing close together, his arm draped round her shoulder.

Suddenly there was the high-pitched sound of an approaching plane and Josef's men set fire to straw bales to light the incoming flight path. Through the smoke and flames, a small Lysander taxied in.

The pilot opened the door and called out in the most pukka accent, 'Who's for Blighty?'

'Here,' said Kit quickly as he pushed Liz forward.

Liz glanced back at Emily, who looked her in the face for the first time since the killing.

'I didn't want to do it, Zoe, but . . .' Liz faltered.

Both women were crying as they hugged each other. Liz beckoned Luc over.

'Look after her, Luc,' she said. 'Promise me that nothing will happen to her.'

'I promise,' Luc said solemnly.

Liz turned to Kit and gazed up into his face.

'Well, Liz,' he said.

'Kit?'

There was a pause then he murmured the only words he could think of. 'I love you very much.'

Liz flung her arms around him and he hugged her tight. He kissed her twice on either cheek and held her out at arm's length, to take a final look at her.

'Bonne chance.' Liz whispered and gently touched his face.

The pilot yelled impatiently at Liz to get on board. She climbed up into the plane, and Kit slammed the door shut behind her. Kit, Emily and Luc all waved as the plane taxied, took off and disappeared into the night.

Long after the sound of the Lysander had died away, Kit stared up at the sky. He found himself humming that song by Vera Lynn. He wondered if he and Liz ever would meet again.